TROUBLE

'Philip Ó Ceallaigh is a wonderful writer who dares
to stay loyal to the short-story form. In this superb
collection, the people he writes about are beautifully observed and precisely "fixed". Here is
a master in full control of his material.'
—John Banville

'Ó Ceallaigh leads the reader into spaces that are
at once dream-like and utterly real. These stories
inhabit a dimension all their own.'
—Danielle McLaughlin

'The thrum of danger from Philip Ó Ceallaigh's
new collection, in lines so tight and clean they
might as well be strung to the page with machine
heads, is exhilarating and perception altering.'
—Gavin Corbett

'Taut, tough stories of singular people. I loved them.'
—Wendy Erskine

TROUBLE

– Stories –

Philip Ó Ceallaigh

The Stinging Fly

The Stinging Fly Press
PO Box 6016
Dublin
stingingfly.org

Trouble is first published in May 2021.

2 4 6 8 9 7 5 3 1

ISBN 978-1-906539-86-3

Set in Palatino.

Printed in Ireland by Walsh Colour Print, County Kerry.

Earler versions of some of these stories were originally published—
in some instances under different titles—in *New Irish Short Stories*
(Faber and Faber), *The Dublin Review, Winter Papers* and in *The Stinging Fly*.
'Bells in Bright Air' was broadcast on BBC Radio 4 as
'I Don't Want to Grow Up'.

The Stinging Fly Press gratefully acknowledges the financial support
of The Arts Council / An Chomhairle Ealaíon.

Contents

TROUBLE

Trouble

I once owned a house in Bucharest. The house was positioned on the crest of a hill and at the back of the house, where the hill fell away steeply, was a flagstoned terrace, facing west, overlooking a good stretch of the city. Bucharest is mostly flat, so being on a hill you got a great sense of peace, of floating above it all, especially if you had a drink in your hand, which I often did. When the evening sun fell the whole scene burned up with colour, like the city was on fire. At other times, when the city was covered with haze from heat and pollution, I half-closed my eyes and imagined I was on a tiny island, looking out across a misty sea.

This is how it happened. At the end of the last century I was working in Dublin, for a security company, on night shifts. I guarded a distillery. Your body never adapts to night work. Day sleep is shallow, turns you dull and sluggish. Winter came, and the sun would be going down as I was getting out of bed. During those long nights I would walk through the warehouses and offices and the cavernous empty canteen with all its vacant tables and chairs and I imagined sometimes I was the last person left on earth. Towards dawn my shoulders would ache just from the strain of staying awake.

On Friday mornings, coming off my shift, I'd pick up my pay. The company offices were at the back of a strip club. They'd be mopping the floor as I walked through the club, with the sad red lightbulbs and the mirrors and the little stage with the pole. One morning, a heavy-lidded man in his fifties with grizzled wavy grey hair was sitting in one of the booths reading a book. This seemed a peculiar thing to be doing in a deserted strip club at dawn, with the smells of cleaning products and the lights on full. When I saw the title—*A Hundred Years of Solitude*—I had to laugh. For months I'd been working. It was a sleepwalking existence and I had just caught sight of my midwinter zombie face in one of the mirrored columns, grey-skinned and my eyes wide and goofy under the peak of my security guard cap. The man looked up, thinking I was laughing at him. I indicated the book.

'You've read it?'

'Forget that bozo,' I said.

I took a disintegrating paperback from my coat pocket and ripped off the front and back sections, leaving about sixty pages from the middle. I handed these to him. It was the Tolstoy story, *The Death of Ivan Ilyich*. Then I went and got my envelope. They paid cash.

I forgot about the magic realist from the strip club. Then, several nights later, at three in the morning, a black Mercedes with tinted windows pulled up at the distillery, in front of the security hut, and he got out. I went outside and we faced each other through the bars of the massive iron gate. The gate was set on rollers over a ground rail and I had to key in a code to make it open. Our breath was white smoke in the freezing air under the bright lights on poles above the distillery perimeter.

'Open that gate,' he said. 'I want to talk to you.'

I told him it was against the rules.

'Do you know who I am?'

I nodded. I'd figured it out. This was my boss, a man called Garrity from the unlovely burg of Newry. His brother was in the Maze for detonating a device under an armoured car some years earlier. Four British lads were inside. I'd seen the pictures. The vehicle had flown some distance through the air and landed in the middle of a field. Under the Belfast Agreement the brother was looking forward to early release.

Garrity had no idea that opening the gate at that hour would have set off an alarm and I don't know why I didn't tell him. He stared at me for a moment then got back in the car and drove away.

I went back at dawn to the room I rented and as I drifted to sleep on my lumpy mattress I thought how good it would be to be fired, to be able to walk about in the day again like other people. I was like one of those heroes sent to the underworld in order to return to tell the story, except I had got lost down there.

But the next day I was not fired and I began to be a little worried, and on the second night the car pulled up and I went out to the gates again and we faced each other, our breaths steaming.

'Can you drive?'

So I started driving for him. It was all because of *The Death of Ivan Ilyich* that I ended up steering that quiet

Mercedes through Dublin's endless suburbs, night after night. Those suburbs, in the dark, were to me death itself, a medieval purgatory, and Garrity's disembodied voice from the back seat confided to me one time that Ivan Ilyich's death was not terrible in itself. What was terrible about Ivan Ilyich's death was that everyone around him carried on with their games and pretended that his death was not really happening, and that at the root of the cancerous indifference was that his wife had never loved him. Garrity was an insomniac so he got things done in the hours of no traffic. His problem with sleep had also turned him into a reader and provoked tremendous mid-life bouts of thoughtfulness. Thanks to me, Garrity discovered the Russians that winter. I gave him Chekhov's *A Boring Story* and Gogol's *Dead Souls* and Shalamov's tales of the gulag. We'd have strange conversations with long pauses. I made sure to say as little as possible. When he referred to his personal life—his divorce, his children—I said nothing at all. Except for the time I gave him the line from Lermontov:

> *We want eternal love and that's not possible*
> *And the other kind's not worth the trouble.*

I drove him to warehouses and the back doors of clubs and restaurants and sometimes to Dublin port. Whatever people will tell you, Dublin isn't a pretty city. All you need to see is the squalling seagulls in the stink of the port at dawn to know there is something putrid in the fibre of the place that no number of Trinity students with coloured scarves will balance out. There's a skanky heroin trail like rats' footprints in shit along the river by the black swamp where the Viking boats first pulled up and it ramifies out north and south and west into the sprawling suburbs of identical houses that await a Hieronymus Bosch to sweep them together with a broom and paint them in subterranean orange flame—even as the entire country geared up for credit-fuelled boomtime it was rotten. Waves of chemical highs shuddered through the city, amphetamine flickers like forked lightning in the sky, followed by lulls of flat exhaustion and nightmare anxiety that nobody ever mentioned. Often too I'd drive without Garrity and pick up envelopes and packages and deliver them on. I soon figured out that some of his associates had firearms expertise. I'd ended up as a guard because I didn't know how to do anything, and now I was earning good money just by keeping my mouth shut. There were new groups in town, Russians and Lithuanians and Chinese, and these and the old Dublin crime families and the enterprising ex-paramilitaries were doing business with each other. Sometimes there were misunderstandings. Every few days someone was shot. It was usually the Dublin people getting shot. They were the most stubborn about territory and the last to see that things had changed. I much preferred a Chinese face looking in the car window than a Dublin aborigine with a corrugated forehead. The Chinese had followed some system that allowed them to expand globally. The local dregs limped around in tracksuits, waiting to get executed.

And one day Garrity's woman was in my rear-view mirror. She looked very young. Far too young for Garrity. Sometimes I drove the girls from the strip club and at first I thought she was one of them. I wasn't far off. She'd worked for him and then he'd taken her out of there.

And early one morning, as the sun was coming up and the quays began again to bustle with nervous office workers, I picked up a package and instead of bringing it where I was supposed to bring it, I brought it to Garrity's girl, as she had instructed me, in a city centre car park. There I abandoned the black Mercedes and we went to the airport and got on a flight to Milano. We had looked at the upcoming flights and didn't fancy Glasgow or Düsseldorf. In Milano we checked into a nice hotel and spent the next couple of days shopping for clothes and watches and jewellery and paying cash. We were also edgy as hell, and we burned off most of the energy in bed. For a week we did nothing but shop and fuck. We'd walk around loaded with money and as soon as we got back to our room we'd open the safe to check the rest was still there. After four days we were worn out from screwing and sweating about the money. Then she had a great idea. We would go to the Black Sea coast, where she was from, sink it in property. She talked like it was Monte Carlo—sea and sun, casinos and tourists. We arrived on a steaming day in early June. The roads were dusty and cratered and the whole population slouched and shuffled about in plastic flip-flops like inhabitants of a refugee camp. Ethno-pop blasted out of kiosks at the railway station and from car windows and miserable little bars inhabited by overweight men who had left home in what appeared to be their underwear. Down by the water there were indeed tourists but you had to wonder what they had escaped from. They crowded the beach by the tepid water, the horizon invisible behind a screen of poisonous haze. Even queuing for ice-cream they suffered, pain written on their faces, as though stocks of ice-cream were running dangerously low. Unhappy men stood ankle-deep in the listless shallows and watched bitterly as speedboats and jet skis churned the water white. To the south loomed the great machinery of the port. The city had all the resources to be wealthy but the wealth flowed around and past the urban peasantry, never touching them. The expensive hotel we stayed at was all glitz and air-conditioned chill and no eye contact between guests. In that country, people with any money at all behaved with a mix of insecurity and aggression, like they'd stolen something. Just like us. Relaxing into money is an art. It takes centuries to learn. It takes a place like Milano, where even the train station looks like a cathedral. In other places having money is like inhabiting the scene of a crime.

'I can't stand this place,' I confessed to her, a few days in, so we gave up on seaside fun and went to the capital, to unload the notes on property there instead. I asked if we would look suspicious paying cash. She just laughed at me.

So that was how I ended up in my big house on the hill, on Aleea Suter, near Carol Park. It was nothing special seen from the front. But from the first time I walked through those big empty rooms I received an impression of space and light, which at the back of the house became an expanse of open sky with the city spread out below it. We moved in and I became meticulous with those empty rooms. I would clean them slowly, lovingly. I sanded and varnished wood. I painted and laid out rugs and put plants in pots and watered them. I even chose the curtains. I loved that house, with all its light and clean space. When I wasn't behaving like a gay interior decorator I was out on the terrace at the back, the place where I was finally free to begin to reflect on my life and all that had happened to me. To our right was the crazy toy castle of The House of the People, a dictator's folly, blocky and monstrous. It was several kilometres away, but when the air was clear it looked close enough to throw a rock at. It was one more element in the strangeness of the place, and I contemplated it as I drank, beneath a vast sky where swallows flitted. I drank vodka, very cold, because vodka is clear and it hits you instantly, without tasking the body with the work of digestion, and you can watch it transforming your vision. My heart opened out in strange and extraordinary directions. In the pause between breaths the whole city would tremble in the heat. I got hold of Thucydides and began to read, all day on the terrace, and I felt it strengthening my view of reality. Reading of ancient events, you learned to discern the essential from the ephemeral in human affairs. I no longer had to follow the news because I had identified the recurring themes, could see the wave patterns of human obsessions moving through history, repeating, but invisible to the individual, who is caught up in daily events and in the shortness of life. I also read Tacitus, the *Bhagavad Gita* and *Winnie-the-Pooh*. I became a time traveller, or time anuller, my reveries punctuated by the sweet tinkling of ice cubes in my glass. Becoming more relaxed, I didn't feel the need to fuck so often. She'd come out onto the balcony in the evening and sit down and look at me patiently and I'd pour the drinks and tell her what was on my mind, whether Alcibiades or a riddle from the Upanishads or something about the colour in the sky. Apart from the mosquitoes in the evening, the climate was perfect. Perfect if you didn't have to move, and I just sat out in my boxers, sweating. Like Robinson Crusoe, I was deeply tanned and had grown a beard. The more I sweated and baked my head under the sun, the deeper I travelled into the palace of ideas. She had business of her own and was generally away with the car and I was glad it was going well for her. I came down one morning and a guy with tattoos on his back was doing press-ups in my living room. This was her cousin, Elvis. Elvis would be staying with us for a while. He gripped my hand and showed his teeth as sweat dripped from his nose. At this point in my life I'd seen enough small-time gangsters to have reservations about Elvis. Still, it was a surprise when she sat down that evening in September—it was still hot and the skies were beautiful above the polluted city—and told me I would have to get out. She explained that Elvis wasn't really her cousin and the house was in her name, as was the car. Indeed, I had let her take care of all the signatures. It was her country. She did the talking and was very competent and I was always pleased to let her get on with it.

I hadn't done it for the money. I had done it to be with her.

Elvis was nice about it. He offered to drop me off any place I liked in the car. I told him it was okay, I felt like walking.

So I left my books behind and descended the hill from the house that had never been mine, into the incomprehensible streets. I had floated above them for months, an angel on a cloud. I had no place to go. If I went back to Dublin, I really would end up winged and haloed. By the people waiting there to shoot me. And suddenly the weather began to change and I understood that I was not in the tropics after all. Temperatures plummeted and the frigid wind stripped the leaves from the trees and the city turned the colour of ash and switched from languorous dilapidated Havana to bombed-out Stalingrad. I was staying at a cheap old hotel near the railway station, on Strada Buzesti—they've demolished it now, to widen the road—and the day my money ran out it was very cold indeed. I had no winter clothes. My hair and beard were matted and the simplest solution was just to shave it all off, and this I did at the little hand-basin in my room that I also used to spare myself the long excursions to the breezy bathroom at the end of the corridor. When that was done I looked for a long time at myself in the mirror, foreign and hollow-eyed, with a prison-camp skull. The gulag effect was only heightened by the striped cotton pyjamas I wore—salvage from my Milano spree. I lay on my back in my room and for long hours contemplated these unexpected changes. I concluded that love never dies. It just moves along and sets up house where it can. Then they threw me out of the hotel. I was walking through the town with a little bag on my back, hungry, when I saw a very beautiful nineteenth-century villa and workmen moving about. The foreman gave me a sledgehammer. I was elated to have work again.

I got a room at the edge of the city in an area called Titan on the tenth floor of a communist block and when it rained I had to put out pots and dishes to catch the drips. My next-door neighbour was a big simple girl from the country called Lili with extraordinary breasts. Her husband, she said, used to beat her until she spat blood. He had run off to Italy and was living with a countess. She told me a lot of stuff and it was mostly lies. She said she loved me, which might have been true, and for that reason wouldn't let me wear a condom, and tried to persuade me to ejaculate in her, which I never felt like doing. And I was heading off every day to the site. The owner wasn't allowed demolish the villa in its present good condition, so he had us rip out the windows and doors and pull up floorboards and bash holes in the interior walls and generally let the weather in. I was never going home and I didn't think about the future. There was no way I could have known then that six years later a motorbike would pull up at a red light beside Garrity's car and that the passenger would shoot him in the head through his open window—the Russians, apparently; the brother had got out of jail and immediately picked a disagreement with them. I'd go back in the evening and often end up drinking with Lili and hear how all kinds of billionaires and geniuses were trying to seduce her. Lili had a leopardskin-print sofa cover and an amazing collection of cuddly toy animals—elephants, rabbits, bears, a giraffe, a penguin, a lion, a tiger, E.T. the Extra-Terrestrial, and a Tyrannosaurus Rex. She also had the first completely shaved pussy I'd ever seen—this was before it became so prevalent—and one evening after a hard day vandalising the nation's patrimony I was begging her on my knees as she stood before me naked except for thigh-high shiny black high-heeled boots to let me rub my face against it—I just couldn't get over how *smooth* that thing was. That day we had been smashing up the roof of the building, all those old red tiles, and just as we were finishing up it began raining heavily, pouring in over the rafters and all the way down into the interior of the building, over the clean white plaster walls and the decorative mouldings, over the remaining floorboards. At that point the owner arrived and stood there, admiring the progress. When I got home, water was percolating through my own roof, and I put the pots out and washed myself and went next door to Lili's to relax. By then the rain had turned to snow and the whole city was freezing over and that meant my job was gone because the weather could do the rest.

So I'd had a few drinks and there I was, down on my knees in front of her, and she says, Come on, tell me the truth, tell me what you're doing in this country and I'll let you put your face in it. And I embraced her hips and said, it's like this Lili, I stole a million bucks from a gangster and stole his beautiful sweetheart and ran away to the Balkans. I remember her whole body shaking with laughter, her big breasts shaking above me as I tried to jam my face against her crotch—I had my arms clamped around her thighs and she was punching my head and laughing—and all the stuffed animals lined up along the back of the sofa were laughing at me too.

Island

I'd been walking all afternoon in the sun. I reached the house and knelt under the pump and let the cold water pour like a river over my head. I drank, then sat there dizzy in the dirt as the cicadas shook their rattle at the cooling evening. Then I got up and walked across the yard to the hammock, strung between two bent pines, and kicked off my boots and pulled the cork on a bottle of rakia. Settling back and drinking, I stared up at the branches, needled green against the blue. I closed my hot eyes. The swollen sun sank beneath the waves.

I was woken by the scraping of their claws on the flagstones, and saw them there in the dusky light, as though through smoke, these little creatures that wouldn't have come up as high as your knee—copulating. I remained absolutely still. If I moved they could take fright, scarper back into the undergrowth, back into the falling night. They were some kind of animal, some kind of monkey, with long tails. Yet they had curiously beautiful faces and impossibly large eyes—hers long-lashed, with high arching brows. She was on all fours, making tiny panting noises, something between a sigh and a squeak. She danced and sang it, grinding him, grinding her teeth, grinding it out. He was on his knees, spine arched and head thrown back, arms limp pendulums grazing his ankles, the rest of his body taut, straining towards where he was hooked.

They might have been tiny humans, if you forgave the tails.

He began to twitch, and she disengaged and spun around to face him and gripped his cock—huge, in proportion to the rest of him—and worked on him, devouring him, gathering rhythm as the waves in the background began to fizz and roar.

She released it from her mouth, and with the final shakes of her little fist he became a fountain of seed, shooting high through the air. She caught it on the face and in her open mouth. He pumped until it dripped from her. She gave his balls a tickle and he arched his back and shot the last of it.

He stood up, tottering—she was rubbing it on herself, convulsing with what I took for laughter—and toppled over. He lay there, his back to me, chest heaving, tail twitching. She leapt to her feet and danced around his body, hopping on one foot then the other. Then she tap-danced, slapping her soles on the flagstones before his face, and back-somersaulted so fast into the darkness that a faint blur hung in the air afterwards, like smoke.

He lay there as though asleep, but I supposed he was listening to the tremor of the waves on the rocks, rising through the earth, through the cut stone where his skull rested. Slowly, slowly, he raised himself on his little elbow and gazed into the night, tail twitching, shot through with electricity, like a cat hit in its dreams by the shadow of a bird passing overhead. He got to his feet and limped away, to disappear between the vines.

I lay very still. The pounding of the waves was a dull thunderous echo in my ears.

Then I moved too, slowly, recalling my body.

The hammock lurched as I reached for the bottle. I raised it to my eyes; it was almost full.

The yard before my house, lit now only by a candle burning in a lamp hanging on a nail on the gable wall, swayed and settled as I lay back, cradling the bottle. I could not remember having lit the candle. It had still been bright when I had lain down. A bat swooped and flitted and was gone again into the darkness. I took a pull from the bottle and it burned down into my gut, into my blood.

Then, from far away, from across the waves of the bay, over the headland, the breeze carried the sound of the church bells. I counted them off, and then it was just me again, and the sea.

*

I had arrived about a month before the thing with the monkeys occurred.

The old man met me where the ferry docked, on the side of the island that faces the mainland. I boarded his skiff. People crowded the quayside, disembarking, and we were already heading out to sea again, rounding a headland, leaving it behind. Seen this way the island was bigger than I had expected. I watched bays and inlets and long stretches of cliff go by. The limestone ridges of the hillsides were pale jutting bones in the evening light. Scrub and small pines clung where they could on the heights. When the sun, which had been hanging over the island when we had docked, was over the sea, I knew we had reached the far side of the island and were approaching our destination. We rounded a point and entered a small rocky cove. He cut the engine and we slid across the water, the slapping of the waves against the skiff audible for the first time. Cigarette pinched in the corner of his mouth, he planted his hand on the wooden post of the jetty and leapt with unexpected litheness. He secured the boat and I rose, stiff from sitting crouched, unsteady as the boat shifted under my weight. He extended an arm and hauled me onto the jetty. I stood there, dizzy at the swaying world, staring out at the dazzling waves. When I turned around I was blind. The world was bleached of detail. All I could discern was the form of the old man, walking away.

We ascended the rough track, me struggling under the weight of my pack, warm breaths of pine and sage and rosemary rising from the baked earth. Then the land opened out in a small plain set in an amphitheatre of hills and a squat house of neatly cut stone came into view, high narrow stone chimney poking from its roof of limestone slabs. Heavy flagstones paved the yard in the front of the house. Woody shrubs had taken root in the cracks between the stones of this rough veranda and some had grown large. All around were neglected fruit trees and vines, the grapes in dense unripe clusters.

He turned a key in the cracked wooden door and forced it open with his shoulder and I followed him inside. He moved through the cool gloom, opening windows and shutters, letting in light. It was a single room with a narrow iron-frame bed set against the far wall. From a wooden trunk he extracted a pile of blankets and dumped them on the bed. He indicated a metal tub and a lump of brownish soap. There was a small stove and a stack of logs on the ground beside it. He opened a dresser and showed me old pots and plates and my provisions: a large jar of cloudy olive oil, a big sack of rice, cornmeal and beans, a large dusty demijohn of red wine and several bottles of rakia. He wiped a couple of cups with his sleeve, uncorked the wine and poured. He handed me a cup, clanked his own against it, and downed it. I drank too, thirstily.

We went outside, to the pump. He worked the handle. It gushed brown water. When it ran clear he had me work the handle while he threw water over his face.

He stood upright, shaking droplets from his hands.

We gazed down the wild slope, past the tangled vines, through the trees, to where a red sun hung low over open sea. The cove had sunk into shadow but further out the water still sparkled brilliantly, a trembling of such terrible intensity you knew it could not long endure. Towards the horizon was a smaller island, flat and monochrome against the bright water, like a paper cut-out. The old man raised his open palms then let his arms flop to his sides. A gesture that seemed to translate as *What more can you ask for?* I felt he was mocking me. It was time to hand over the money. He counted it, nodded, folded the wad and put it in his back pocket. He took his cigarettes from his shirt pocket and offered me one. I accepted, though I no longer smoked. Soon I would be alone, and it would be dark. We smoked together for a moment, looking at the sea. This is what people do, I thought. They look upon open spaces, where light falls. Then he turned and pointed to a place beside the house where a hammock hung between two pines, and spoke one word.

He nodded to me in farewell, and was already descending the path. Soon he was lost from view. I continued smoking in the gloom.

I tossed the butt. It hissed briefly where the water from the pump had pooled in the dirt.

I stood there for a long time. I thought of the dark house and lighting the stove. Then I remembered the hammock, and the wine. I brought out the demijohn and set a big log there as a table beside the hammock and settled in. I drank a glass. And then another. One by one the stars came out. I smothered my hunger in wine.

*

Next morning I ate from the apricot and fig trees. The earth beneath the branches was stained in dark patches where the ripe fruit had fallen and burst. Then I set to work. I ripped the weeds and shrubs from between the cracks in the flagstones. I hoed the hard earth between the rows of vines, clearing the wild growth choking the plants. I pruned the vines. When it became too hot to work, I sat in the shade and admired my tidy patch of cultivated land, the broken soil with the tinge of moisture showing darker against the pale baked earth. Even as I watched, it was drying to the same dusty colour. It was rocky land, mostly. Evidence of the struggle to subdue it was written there. Great mounds of rock were stacked on the hillsides and ran along the slopes in long lines. On the gentler gradients, these deposits of rock narrowed and became the walls of terraces, sculpting the land neatly. At one time, it must have been a garden. But the terraces were overgrown now, and collapsing. Working alone, I could only hope to tame the level area around the house.

In the cooling evening, I went down to my cove. Fish swam in the clear water among the rocks. I experimented with baits and cast out with the handreel. But I could only reel in crabs. They hung stupidly in the air, dripping water in molten beads, clamped obstinately to their prey even as they became prey themselves. The fish ignored me, but the crabs kept coming. I kept the three biggest. Back at the house I boiled them with rice, smashed the claws and extracted the scraps of flesh.

*

But time was out of joint even before the fuck-monkeys came.

I had lost track of the days, but always counted off the bells from the church, when I could hear them. They became irregular. They would toll two and the next time four. Or toll the same number of times on two consecutive hours—I presume they were hours—and I did not know if the second occasion was a mistake or the rectification of a previous error. Errors in the stone tower of the church? I was untroubled, even when the shadows nudging across the yard stopped and slowly receded again, for maybe an hour. What did I care, junked out on its rays, if the sun rolled backwards? What did I care about the giant spider spinning between the trees? All you want is one day, beneath the sun, like a butterfly.

My glass would refill when I was busy meditating on the insects in the grass and at first I supposed I had lost the capacity to track the true sequence of events. I'd drain the strong red wine, enter my house to look for a knife perhaps, or a piece of string, and when I returned, my glass, which I'd left drained on the stump by the hammock, was brimming so full I'd have to stoop down and slurp at it ungracefully.

I decided to test it, one day. I drained the glass, took a good hard look at it, said, I'm watching you. When I came back after gutting some fish it was still empty. It only refilled when my mind was elsewhere.

But as long as the monkeys, or whatever it was, were refilling my glass, giving me more hours not less, I was happy to go along with the joke. My work was coming along. I had a stretch of well-tended vines and the grapes were swelling with their juice, and in the rows between I had the beginning of corn, tomatoes, beans and peppers, and my fishing was improving. I rose at dawn, splashed water on my face, then worked among my plants. I had made mistakes in the past, on the mainland. The why of things had not been revealed to me. And so I was patient on the island.

Then, dozing in my sling, the bottle nearby, I would hear the scratching of their claws on the flagstones, and half open my eyes. The monkeys began to come like this regularly, and always when my mind was elsewhere. Sometimes they fucked with tenderness, sometimes anger, but always afterwards he was alone, and it seemed he remembered what it was he had gone there to forget. He would fall and lie with his skull against the flagstones and his little ribcage—rabbit ribs, fishbones—would protrude with each ragged breath. He'd drag himself into the tunnel of darkness between the vines and I'd reach for my bottle and take a long pull.

And I recalled the old man, that first day, pointing, saying one word. I couldn't be sure I remembered exactly what it was.

*

I had turned away from the cities of the mainland, where they love what is worthless and worship what is false. That part of my life was over. The good man is a tree that grows beside a stream, tall and straight, and gives fruit at the chosen moment. But I grew curious to see what was over the promontory, to see the town from where the sound of the bells came when the east wind blew. Eventually I would have to go there. I was not yet producing enough to eat.

And I had nothing left to drink, even with the refills.

I set off, empty bottles rattling in my pack. The spiders had been spinning in the cool of morning. The webs between the branches of the trees and the bushes were strung with tiny pearls of moisture and I slashed ahead with a stick to clear the way. The path climbed gently, following the promontory's seaward stab, and as the sun gathered strength the dew burned off and the smell of pine and rosemary was carried on the warm breeze. The sea swelled vaster and brighter with each step upwards, the light breaking and scattering on the wavetops, and when I looked back I could see my home and the evidence of my work and striving; a tiny patch of order suspended in the infinite wildness of earth and wave and sky. And each time I looked back it was smaller, and dearer to me. Then it was gone and I was high above the world and cresting the promontory, keen to see what lay beyond.

As the track peaked, the vista of an immense bay opened on the far side. Set there, in the distance, where the steep hills met the water, was the town, with its harbour and fort and the steeple that rang the distant bells that came to me on the wind. I removed my pack and sat on a rock and caught my breath and gazed.

It was a Venetian town of clean-hewn stone, a point on the trade with Ragusa and Constantinople. Perhaps it had seen Turks and Crusaders in its time, before settling into the era of peace. I imagined fig and lemon trees growing in tidy gardens in the outskirts, bees bumbling in the lavender and oleander, the narrow alleys of the town centre, the high windows and heavy doors of the houses of merchants. There would be wide quays, fishing boats swaying in a forest of masts, men conversing in the cafés.

Having rested, I rose and put on my pack and continued along the path, the town glittering ahead of me. But then I stopped and turned back and sat again upon a rock, head in my hands, undecided. When I stood up again my bottles clanked and I felt foolish and cowardly. I had to buy provisions.

My progress was next stopped when I sighted a small boat in the bay. I could not be sure at first, but then it appeared to me to be the old man, on course to round the promontory. I turned and hurried back, running at times, to arrive at the bay, or at least the house, before he could.

I reached the house, sweating, breathing hard, and unloaded the bottles from the pack. I wished to hide what I had been about to do. I met him down at the cove, unloading supplies onto the jetty. He laughed when he saw me—my beard was now as long as his—and seemed better disposed to me than the first time. And I was glad to see him. I had seen nobody since coming to the island. He had brought wine and rakia, rice and flour and oil, matches and candles, and jars of olives and capers and honey. With a stubby pencil he scratched out a sum on the boards of the jetty, listing each item. It meant the end of my money, almost. We carried the supplies up towards the house.

He took in my improvements with grudging admiration. Some of the grapes were ripe already and we cut a load, which I bartered against the price of the flour.

I fetched two cups and we sat on logs on the veranda and drank.

I pointed to the hammock and spoke the three-syllable word he had said that day. He shook his head. I repeated it, trying variants, putting the stress on different places. His face hardened, and he shook his head. This was an act. He knew well what I was referring to, pointing to the hammock and the place near the vines where the monkeys would appear.

He shook his head and rose. I rose also, tossing the last drops of rakia from my cup onto the ground. There was nothing I could do if he would not talk. We carried the grapes down to the jetty, not speaking. I went back up to the house and began to drink the wine.

*

The weeks passed in work, and my grapes were swelling and becoming sweet, and were particularly abundant in the area closer to the house, where I had worked hardest. But I had no way to transport the ripe fruit. I had no boat and going by foot over the headland was too laborious. And I had no barrels, or experience in making wine. A small mistake would ruin everything.

I would need help, and that meant dealing with the town. In the meantime, I carried on working.

I'd drink wine, the moon would rise, and I'd fall asleep in the hammock and dream intricate scenes where the actors swapped masks and voices. Impossible cities, tunnels and trains and staircases and corridors. Money that disintegrated as you went to buy the ticket. Broken phones. Guards that demanded the password that you had on a scrap of rag, ink washed out with the rain. Maps that grew and shifted beneath your eyes. The key dropping through the bars of the drain in the crowded street. The impossibility of ever getting home, of ever coming to rest; only the endless trials of the endless road, the purpose of the journey misconceived. Dreams where your teeth crumbled in your mouth and your hair fell out. Dreams that resembled life. One night I woke in the hammock from my troubled visions, my mouth dry from wine, to the scratching of their claws on the stones. I opened my eyes and saw the stars as a spray of luminous dust, as they appear only in parched and blacked-out lands where you are utterly alone.

I turned my head, and saw that they were three; the new one thick-necked and brutish, short wiry hair covering his body, slouching insolently. The first male was tugging at the arm of the female, entreating her, as she glanced towards the brute. This went on for some time, the brute lying on the ground on his side, leaning on one elbow, picking at his teeth with a twig. Once he turned to look at the lovers, and spat. The first male tried to embrace the female, to kiss her shoulder and neck, but she was writhing away from him. She broke free and hissed at him, baring her teeth, and he struck an open-handed blow that knocked her tottering sideways, clutching her face, whining in pain and anger. He stood over her, fists bunched, ready to do it again. She glanced at the brute, who was now paying attention. He tossed away the twig and slowly, heavily, got to his feet and lumbered over to them. It looked choreographed and inevitable. There was no contest, but the smaller male had to see the scene through. The blow—a swift uppercut to the chin—sent him sailing through the air. His head hit the flagstones with a crack and he lay sprawled, out cold, legs splayed, arms in the crucifixion position. The brute turned to the female. Her resistance was token. He forced her down and got her legs apart. It seemed to cause her some distress at first, but then she got the hang of it. It was a different kind of mating to what she'd entered into with the little fellow, each thrust shunting her back across the ground. The muscles across the brute's back tensed. He grunted and slumped, pinning her beneath him. Then he disengaged and got to his feet as she lay there, looking soft and bruised. He picked her up, threw her over his shoulder and walked away, into the leafy darkness beneath the vines.

Slowly, the little monkey climbed to his feet. His tail twitched uncontrollably. Looking all the time at the ground, he hobbled in the direction the others had gone.

When I could no longer see him and it was entirely still again, I reached for my glass, on the tree stump beside my hammock. It was full to the brim, though I could not remember having filled it.

*

The work continued, and I became concerned about the grapes, troubled that all I had laboured for should fall to the dust and rot, when it might become good wine, something to store and to savour. Yes, it was the wine pulling me back to the world, the swelling grapes demanding to be picked and pressed, me wandering the rows, knowing I would soon have to go back over the promontory and ask for help. The summer was at its peak and I could already foresee the grey days of winter, the cold rain gusting in from the sea, me shivering by the stove in the house. I was thinking about the future again.

*

The sun went down on our world of trouble and the moon rose red and I sipped the dark wine and my eyes rolled back in my head. When they opened again the stars were singing and there was sound on the wind like the tinkling of windchimes. The stars blurred and swam about the sky like little silver fish. I turned my head and there he was, the brute, riding a little red open-top motor car, one hand on the wheel, elbow of the free arm resting on the door, the female in the passenger seat. It was an old model, big round headlights, all curves, and he was making circles and figures of eight in this toytown machine. Beyond, towards the vines, a party was going on, the creatures—monkeys, little people, I no longer knew—were swarming in and out of the shadows of the plants. It was lively around the bar, the males trying to attract the interest of the females, a lot of fooling around, tugging and shoving, strutting and dancing. One little fellow was doing magic tricks, finding coins behind the ears of a female. I spotted the male I knew from before, the one who took the beating, and he was on the hard stuff, propping up the bar, while behind him a bartender was mixing cocktails, throwing bottles in the air and catching them behind his back with his tail, that kind of thing. And over the buzzing of the little car's motor the tinkling and ringing was getting louder, mixing with other sounds, becoming music, and a swing band was braiding through the vines in procession, the horn notes punching through the night, the tails of the players swaying to the beat. Finally all these little creatures were through—the bass cellist, struggling to keep up, came in last. The car screeched to a stop and the brute and his monkey-girl jumped out and started jiving. The monkeys at the bar were all shaking it, the whole joint jumping to the rhythm, the ground itself shaking to the beat. The barman was showing off, dancing about with the cocktail shaker in his hand like a maraca. The little drunken monkey remained alone at the bar. He tried clicking his fingers but his rhythm was long gone and his foot slipped from the footrest and he nearly toppled over. The tune ended, the brass section dipped their instruments and an accordionist and a fiddle player stepped forward and struck up a tango. The dancefloor turned serious, even the brute straightened up and threw his head back, took his partner's hand and pranced her across the floor. They leaned into each other, moving as a single being, her doing little decorative sidesteps and drawing little circles and half-circles and *ochos* in his orbit. The sad monkey drank and watched. When the end of the melody came, the crowd cheered the brute and his sweetheart, and he leapt into the driver's seat, over the car door, and flicked hers open. She got in and they did a final circuit of the assembly, her waving as they applauded, and accelerated into the night. The party began disintegrating after that. Monkeys were getting more evident in their lasciviousness, pairing off, and there were some nasty little scuffles, mean but brief, to establish who got whom. The bar was shutting up and the musicians were moving off in a line, playing 'When the Saints Go Marching In'. They twined in and out of the grapevines until lost to sight, the sounds becoming smaller and smaller, the tinkling windchimes of the stars ringing again in my ears with the chatter of the cicadas in the hot still air of the summer night—and I could remember the words from somewhere:

> *Some say this world of trouble*
> *Is the only one we need*
> *But me, I'm waiting for that morning*
> *When the new world is revealed*
>
> *Oh when the saints…*

All that was left of the party finally was the wounded little monkey, lying on his side, tail limp and lifeless with drunkenness. I reached for my brimming glass and drained it, spilling half in my beard, then I rolled out of the hammock and hit the ground. Don't worry, monkey, I said, as the stars waltzed round my head, I'll save you. But I appeared unable to rise. I was glued to the ground. I lifted my arm but the earth's gravitation was more than usually strong and my arm slapped back down. My legs and my head had no better luck.

I awoke and the ground was shaking. The stars were blown out and I could hear the vines and trees whipping and tossing like they feared to be torn apart in the wind and the rain. The clay beneath my face had turned to mud. My bare feet splashed through puddles as I stumbled to the house. Inside was pitch darkness. I felt my way to the cot in a dream, and collapsed.

*

Dead things are heavier. You sense when you pick up a living creature in your hands how little it weighs. A cat weighs nothing at all when alive. You feel when you hold its warm springy body that this is a creature that darts up trees, flies across rooftops. A dog too, even a big one, if standing, can be scooped up easily and will seem light. It's different when life has fled from the flesh. And so it was the next morning when I picked this tiny creature up from where he lay beneath an awning of vineleaves, on the damp earth. Even though he weighed almost nothing, the surprise was that he weighed anything at all. How is it, I wondered, that he had become real, finally, being dead? And again this life seemed to me a dream, all light and movement, only exposed for what it was by the weight of the dead flesh.

His bones—his ribs and shoulders, the little knots of his joints—protruded terribly. His skin was cold and clammy to the touch and his eyes, like the eyes of any dead creature, be it fish or man, were duller than the stones on the ground. I lifted his corpse in my cupped hands and carried it towards the house and laid him on the flagstones. I went and got an old sack that had contained beans and I ripped the cloth apart to make a shroud and wrapped him inside. I had to bury him so that the remains would not be scavenged by birds and rodents. With my mattock in one hand and the bundle clasped to my body with my other arm, I ascended the path up the hill, high up, past the last of the decaying terraces. The storm had blown itself out, and yet there was still a lot of dirty cloud scooting about, and a breeze was blowing the tops off the waves on the choppy darkened sea. Where my feet kicked the gravel of the path the soil beneath was dark with moisture. Yes, when the sun shone again the earth would put out its greenest shoots, the buds would sense their moment and break into leaf and bloom. It would happen all over again—growth, pollination, the bringing forth of fruit, and its sure decay.

I reached a patch of flat open ground with a pleasant outlook over the terraces below. Higher up, vague mounds and lines of rocks indicated collapsed terraces. Lower down, and abandoned more recently, they gained definition. They became finely wrought geometric shapes just above my house, where I had lovingly cleared the land and tended the soil. The house itself was set in the middle of a swathe of level ground where long straight rows of vines flourished. It looked rich down there. It was my season's work, though I had no idea if I could save it. Perhaps this view was my only reward; my land, and my little bay, and the sea beyond beneath the vast curving sky. I laid the shroud on the ground and began to dig. I hacked and chipped and I levered out stones and rocks until the hole was deep enough, then I laid the bundle inside and began to cover it up, beginning gently with the finer soil and sand, then with the smaller stones, and then with the larger ones, which I tamped down with my foot. Finally, I searched the area for large clean rocks, and when I had enough I began to pile them up. I started with the largest flattest rocks and built up until I was using the smaller stones. I lost track of time, caught up in my work, and when I stepped back at last the grave was a beautiful thing, a gently curved cairn that rose from the land as if part of it, set in that natural clearing, overlooking the world. I had the satisfaction at least that I had acted fittingly. I wiped my dirty hands on my trousers, picked up the mattock by the shaft and went back down towards the house.

As I descended, the clouds broke and the sun shone upon the land, transforming it again. By the time I reached the house the fever was overtaking me. I was cold in the sunshine and sweating. I took the bucket and fetched water. By now every movement was costing me great effort, my limbs were heavy and my mind torpid. With the bucket of water and a ladle by the cot, I lay down and covered myself with all the clothing and blankets I had, and still it was not enough, I sweated and I trembled. And yet it was strangely pleasurable, to be drifting back and forth through sleep and wakefulness, detached from the world, opening my eyes again and seeing that it was still bright day through the door, and it seemed the longest day ever. In my indifference to time and its passage, I might have been awakening to a succession of days, more or less the same. It was unimportant, because all I wished was to lie there and do nothing. I would drift into unconsciousness and I would wake myself with little yelps or shouts that seemed to have no source in anything I could remember imagining or dreaming, but reminded me of a dog when it is disturbed in its dreams. And I recall thinking, every creature is tortured in its dreams, the lowest and the highest, always running, pursued by phantoms, even when stretched out unconscious on the ground. But at last the evening did draw in, very slowly, and the night too was one of sleeping and waking, and all my heavy flesh wished for was to wish for nothing, to lie there, kissed by nothingness.

*

By morning it had mostly passed. I rose and went outside in the growing light and beheld my gardens, my land, the house where I had laboured, and it was all changed. I was free of it. I looked at the full vines and now it meant nothing. It was not my problem.

I had gone to the island to hear only the sounds made by sea and wind and earth, to sustain myself in its grace, to eat what it yielded, gone there to shrug off the nagging frightened flesh, its memory and craving, believing thereby my journey was at an end. But I had understood nothing. The journey never ends. I looked at the vines and saw in the swollen berries the problem I had wrapped myself around and which had tied me there, a dream—like that of the woman and the man in their perfection, each striving towards the other, both towards release, and then falling, knowing it is to begin all over again from the start—and now it mattered no more that the grapes would lie where they fell. There was nothing to be saved. There was always too much fruit, and it rotted where it fell. How had I forgotten that?

The sun rose over the sea and I went to the pump and washed the sweat off myself. The fever had not entirely passed but it was pleasant, the cold water. Then I dressed in clean clothes and put a few things in my sack. I did this without thinking, naturally, because going to the town was what I wanted, in that moment. I'd had all the solitude a soul could take. I wasn't travelling for any reason. I wasn't setting out on a journey. I was just going for a walk.

I picked a bunch of ripe grapes to eat while I walked. I climbed the path along the hillside, eating them, spitting seeds as I went.

Smoke

Wind in my face, I rode the bike hard into the sun, jolting across uneven stubbled earth, engine roaring. Before me— fields beneath enormous sky, the brimming glassy bay, the sand dunes stretched across the far side of the bay a jagged mountain-chain.

I was seventeen years old.

I turned too tight, leaning, wheels slipping from under me, then came upright again, tasting exhaust smoke, in too high a gear, shuddering while I caught speed, and aimed for the open gate to the upper field. Ruts from tractor wheels were parched canyons in the gateway. Rocks poked through the gouged dusty earth. I needed to slow for it. I accelerated.

Passing through the gateway, the world shook me loose.

And then I was staring at the blue empty sky.

I lay there in silence and stillness. I was aware of where I was, and what had happened in the days and weeks preceding that moment. But my troubles no longer belonged to me. They were clamouring little objects I watched from above, free of them, just as I observed the desperation of my body as my throat made foul funny noises, begging for breath. I had heard rumours of the soul, of course, but later I would always know it as that jailbird inside my ribcage, just flown, glancing back at the world as it rose to dissolve itself in the blue. And I wondered if my back was broken.

I heard a groan as the breath entered me, and panicked. The body clutching at me again, pulling me down. The blue was gone. My eyes were squeezed shut and the thought of my broken back was horror. It was the fear of the flesh, pinned to the earth. Someone slapped my leg hard. My head jerked up and my eyes opened. I was alone.

The motorcycle was on its side, back wheel still spinning fast.

I sat up and watched it.

Time was not what I previously believed it to be. I had just stepped out of it.

The wheel slowed and stopped.

I got up, looking around, glad my legs worked. I was still slightly deaf. I was still inhabiting the vision, and wanted to hold on to it a little longer, but breath by breath it slipped away. I looked at the world I was returning to. The bales of straw were arranged in eights, here and there about the field, where I had stooked them. The grain was in the silo, the straw would soon be in the barn. And then we would raze the stubble, trailing burning plastic fertiliser bags across the ground. The bushes and trees and sky would tremble in the heat-haze and drifting smoke as the fire caught and moved in a line across the land.

A couple of weeks before this happened, before I was hurled like a rag doll to the hard earth—and discovered that I was a soul, and that time was just an obsession, a condition, of the body, and that thought itself, compulsive and time-bound, was the fault of the body—I had become a man. She was a couple of years older than me. I was remembering her naked when I accelerated at that wrong moment.

Her family was away that afternoon, and I'd ridden the bike into town. In the kitchen she gave me beer and offered me a cigarette. I looked at it and shook my head. I'd never smoked. She smoked a lot. I liked that about her. I liked everything about her. I wanted to kiss her. I'd kissed girls before, but never sober during the day.

—Say something, Space.

They called me Space. It had been Spaceman once. I moved under another gravity, like a moonwalker.

I shrugged and drank some beer.

I tried hard to think of something to say, but nothing happened. It was like the thing with the chickens; someone had done an experiment, putting food on the other side of their wire. They crowded together, squawking like crazy, looking at the food. It was discovered that really hungry chickens would starve to death even if the gate to the run was left open—they couldn't tear their eyes from the food. Less hungry chickens would go for a stroll and eventually stumble across their dinner. Which drove the starving chickens on the other side mad.

I couldn't relax and talk properly. I wanted too much to kiss her.

—I never know what you're thinking about, she said.

I told her about the chicken experiment. She listened patiently, nodding from time to time, smoking, and said:

—You're great company, Space.

She walked out of the kitchen. I felt ashamed. I looked at her cigarettes on the table. Maybe it was time to try one. I could hear her in the other room. I followed her. She was looking out the window at the back garden, smoking. I stood beside her. I wondered if she wanted me to leave. She extinguished her cigarette and said:

—What do you want to do?

I shrugged and said:

—Drink some beers. Whatever you want to do is fine.

She turned and walked away, down the hall. I watched her go, beautiful and severe, long black hair swaying. She went into a room. I could hear her doing something.

I went back into the kitchen. She'd left her cigarettes on the table. I looked at them. I finished the beer. I took another from the fridge and opened that and took a drink. I brought it with me down the hall, quietly, and looked into the room she'd entered. I couldn't see her. It was dim. The curtains were pulled. I took several small steps into the room. She was in bed, under the covers, looking at me.

—What's wrong? I whispered. Are you sick or something?

—Take your clothes off.

I put my beer on the dresser and took my clothes off and got in beside her.

It was different, kissing someone and our naked bodies touching and hands moving all over. Many things were happening at once. No wonder, I thought, this is so popular.

—Your cock is very big.

—Yeah.

—No, I mean, compared to other men.

I'd never been called a man before. It didn't bother me about the other cocks she was familiar with. Their owners were away in other places—working in petrol stations and farms and warehouses, or sitting in bars and kitchens—and it was mine she was gripping now.

—Is it a problem?

—Let's find out.

—I don't have a condom.

It wasn't strictly necessary, she said. She explained how it worked. It sounded easy. But still, what if…

—You want to do it or not? she demanded.

Afterwards, we sat in the kitchen again. She offered me a cigarette. I shook my head. She lit up and smoked.

—Why are you looking at me like that? she asked.

—Can we do it again?

—Right now?

—Sometime.

She laughed.

—You're great company, Space.

She finished her cigarette. I finished my third beer.

—Well, you'd better get out of here, or they'll be carrying you out.

Indeed, I seemed to be melting, slumping down into the chair. I did as I was told, getting to my feet. I felt pretty good. Relaxed but light.

She walked me to the front door and opened it. I went out and got on the bike. I didn't have a helmet. Tax or insurance either. Or a licence. She was at the edge of town. It was open country through to where I lived.

I rode homewards, sun on my face.

I stood up and looked around. The sky was cloudless. The bay was still brimming, the tide on the point of turning. I was unhurt. I was in no hurry to get back to the world of doing and thinking and feeling. I pulled the bike upright and examined it. It seemed fine. I got on and kick-started it. It turned first time and I rode it gently up to the house.

It was an old house, two storeys, painted white, built in the nineteenth century. There was a giant fireplace in the living room, big enough that you could stand in it. My father had been born in that house. I rode the bike into the courtyard and parked it. There were stables and outhouses, plastered and painted white also. In places the plaster had fallen off, revealing red brick. Nobody was home. And in the silence after the engine died I looked at the house and I understood what was going to happen. I had never envisaged the future before except in vague daydreams and longings, but now it presented itself as a fact, another aspect of my sudden lucid vision, another thing I would be able to tell no one, except when it had already come to pass: that this house would one day be a ruin. My parents would be gone from it, my brothers and sisters would be gone, the old trees would be cut down, the roof would fall in and a tree would grow from the floorboards in the room where my parents had slept. Everything before me now that was whole would be undone, and I would live to see it.

It was Sunday and it was silent and still because everyone was away at the statues. Statues of the Blessed Virgin had begun to move, to gesture to the faithful. It had started down the coast from us, in Ballinspittle, and now statues in townlands all over the country were moving. The believers would congregate to kneel and pray, day and night, in every weather, staring, awaiting her next sign. News and talk shows brought the latest reports; a group of Donegal maidens walking home from an evening's set dancing had seen a light in the sky above a hedgerow and the face of Our Lady appeared and told them to prepare themselves for the coming message. The land trembled on the brink of revelation.

So I entered the living house that day seeing that it would one day be a ruin, alone with my vision, because the folks were away, expecting bigger news.

I went up to my room. It was dim and ghostly after the brightness of the open country. Through the window I could see the flat-topped Comeraghs out to the west. I wished I was walking on their heights, from where you could see half the world. A slowly growing crack of anxiety had appeared in the perfection of my earlier mood. I sat down on the bed and rubbed my eyes. Then I picked up the book lying open on the bed. I had been reading it that morning but could remember nothing of it. I looked at the page and the lines jumped out at me:

> *Just as a reservoir is of little use when the whole*
> *Countryside is flooded, the illumined man*
> *Has little need of scriptures, seeing as he does*
> *Divinity in everything around him.*

I heard an engine I recognised and I stood up, dropping the book to the floor.

I went down. Joe was standing in the yard by the bike in his *Top Gun* pose, helmet under one arm, feet planted apart. His long curly hair already springing back. Around his neck he wore a red and white Palestinian headscarf. He was a year older than me.

—Howya, Space. Quiet round here. Isn't it?

—They're away at the statues. Mount Mellory. The ma says she feels something is going to happen.

He took out his cigarettes, put one in his mouth, and lit a match, looking at me:

—You know? I fucken wish it would.

He leaned into the flame, then looked at me again and said, smoke spilling from his mouth:

—What's the matter with you?

I shook my head. I couldn't tell him anything. It didn't seem possible.

—You look like you've been sniffing solvents.

I shrugged.

—Well. I won't beat about. S'pose you heard already.

—No, I lied.

—G-wan-ya-did.

I said nothing. He took a couple of puffs in short succession, looking at me, maybe trying to figure me out.

—It's like this. It happened and I'm more surprised than anyone. Well. There you have it.

I nodded. He didn't need to say her name. It was there already.

—I wanted to tell you, to your face. Because I know you used to like her.

—I still do like her, Joe.

—Sure why wouldn't you, she's a good one.

—Yeah.

At this point the crows in the trees around set off on one of their panics and I looked up at them and thought something would happen. And Joe looked up but already they were starting to settle and he thought less of it and it was over soon, except for some squawking.

—I know you had a thing for her, so… Out of respect… No hard feelings.

I shook my head.

—Well, Space, you're alright. It's a load off, to talk to you. I suppose you want to know how it happened.

—No.

—We were drinking, the gang of us, down at the sand dunes, and I walked off and lay down and was looking at the sky. I just seemed to wake up and she was on top of me. There I was, looking up at the stars and getting my hole. And drunk as I was, boy, I remembered you were into her. I thought of you. But it was too late anyway.

—Ah, sure.

—It was a good ride. Very natural, finding a young one on top of your knob like that. Pure fucken poetry. The firelight and the stars in the open air and all. But the thing is.

He looked at me meaningfully.

—What is?

—I mean, it's not just getting the ride and all. I really like the girl.

—That's good, Joe.

—Yeah, well, we'll see how it goes. You never can tell.

I nodded. Joe dropped what was left of his cigarette and ground it under his boot.

—Well.

—Give us a smoke there.

—Yeah.

He tapped out a Camel and I took it. I put it in my shirt pocket. He didn't comment, though he knew I never smoked.

—You're fucken all right, Space, so you are.

I couldn't argue. It was his film.

—Can I have the matches too?

He handed them over. He put on his helmet and got on and kick-started the bike. It was a powerful machine, unlike mine. I had a big cock, though. Then again, I'd only really used it once and it hadn't brought me luck. We waved goodbye and Joe took off. I watched him go. Then I stood there, listening to him accelerating down the road, ripping the gentle countryside apart with his noise. I wandered over to the chicken run and gripped the wire and stared in at the hens.

It got dark and late and still I was on my own. Something must be going on at the statues, perhaps the Second Coming, and I was the last soul in the country to hear about it. They were living pages from the Book of Revelation, while I was tormented by images of firelight orgies at the sand dunes, naked bodies leaping and dancing and copulating among the flames. I wandered from silent room to silent room, still with the vision in my mind of the house as a ruin. I opened a cabinet and drank from a bottle of my father's whiskey. He didn't mind me doing that. I don't mind you getting drunk, he told me once, as long as you're not smoking marijuana. People smoked it, he explained, and jumped off buildings, thinking they could fly. I started to feel like the last human being alive on earth. What if they had all ascended on a pillar of light, clutching their rosary beads? I couldn't stay still. There was nothing left of the peace I felt when I came off the bike.

I went out to the yard and paced about in the dark. What I had to do was walk.

I went around the house and through the front gate and down the road, between the dark hedgerows. I emptied the bottle and sent it sailing into the night. It landed with a soft clunk. The stars were out and a sliver of a moon. I walked fast, trying to think of nothing. Then I heard a car engine from very far away. Finally the light from its headlights became visible, then the bright headlights themselves as it rounded a curve and came towards me.

It pulled up beside me. A police car.

The guard at the wheel rolled his window down. There was another one in the passenger seat and another in the back.

—Howya. Late in the evening to be out for a walk?

—What time is it?

—Late. Where are you going?

—Nowhere.

He frowned. He asked my name and address. I told him.

—Don't believe you. I don't believe you're from round here at all. Who's your neighbours?

I gave them Dalys, Hanleys, Mulcahys and Doyles. Walshes, Powers, Chasteys and Phelans. Meades, Quinlans and Quirkes. I gave them half the county.

—That's enough, you blaggard. Who's your parish priest?

I gripped the car door and leaned towards the cop and told him, loudly, to his face:

—JUST AS THERE IS LITTLE NEED OF A RESERVOIR WHEN THE ENTIRE COUNTRYSIDE IS FLOODED, THE ILLUMINED MAN HAS LITTLE NEED OF PRIESTS, SEEING AS HE DOES THE LORD IN ALL AROUND HIM!

The clicking of three car doors opening together, a rumble of bogman curses, and I was already leaping the iron gate into the field behind me. I sprinted into the darkness, tripping and falling and rolling and laughing and getting up again and running again. I heard sheep bleating somewhere and the pounding of all the little hoofs and it sounded so funny I found it hard to run with the laughter. I could see the shadows of the trees in the hedgerows against the relative brightness of the sky, dusted with stars, and I made for that, knowing the field was bordered with deep drainage trenches. I looked back and could see the torch beams flash erratically between ground and sky as the cops hauled themselves over the gate. I slid down the steep side of the drainage trench, coming to a splashing stop in ankle-deep water, boots sinking in weeds and silt on the bottom. The frogs went wild. A chain reaction of frog-hysteria. I held my sides to stop laughing. Snot was hanging out my nose. I looked up at the stars and wanted to howl—the frogs were going jabba-wabba, and the cops were in hot pursuit, shouting hilarious stuff about me only making it worse for myself, their thrashing torch beams detonating the branches of the trees above me in joyous flashes—and the sheep weren't bleating any more, they were squealing, having heart attacks, sure their throats would be cut.

I experienced that breakneck urge I'd had that afternoon on the bike, the temptation to call out to the cops to come and get me. I imagined scrambling through the hedgerows and into the next field and taking them cross-country. But I thought better of it. The hedgerow was probably too dense to penetrate. They'd seize me in the drainage ditch and we'd splash about like overexcited pigs, their flailing arms making a mudwrestling light show, then they'd haul me out and give me a good kicking.

So I hugged my sides and held in my laughter. Finally the lights stopped flashing about and I heard the clanging of them clambering over the metal gate, muttering to each other. I heard the engine starting, and the car driving away, the noise very clear in the night air, an enormous sound, even as it changed and became distant. I held onto it until I could hear it no more and still I stood there. The frogs were settling down again. It would be as well to stay there with them for a while, and when returning along the road to take shelter at the sound of any vehicle. I was an outlaw now.

It became very quiet. My feet in the water, I gazed up at the unblinking stars. I could feel the cold water, but I was hardly a body any more. Ever since coming off the motorbike, I hadn't quite settled back into it. I was no longer something solid, I was dissolved in that vast blackness, and I felt my breathing and my heartbeat and the tingling of my skin as a vibration, a faint tremor, just like the trickling of the water in the drainage ditch and the whisper of the leaves in the air above me.

I was crying then. I wonder why my body is crying, I thought, because I feel fine here in the drainage ditch. Those were tears, and my chest was shuddering. But that had happened too when I was laughing, moments before. Soon I couldn't tell whether I was laughing or crying. I had been so wound up over the past weeks, wound up in my trouble, and I was exhausted. I had waited so long for my life to begin, and now suddenly this thing with the girl I couldn't understand, and standing in the drainage ditch with the frogs. Observe this helpless shaking of the body, I told myself, wiping the snot and tears with my sleeve.

I patted my pocket. The cigarette was there, and the matches. I took out the cigarette and struck a match and illuminated the little world in front of me, and lit the cigarette. I inhaled. I tossed the match and it hissed. I was in darkness again. I stood in the ditch, the water trickling by my feet, and exhaled, looking upwards to the trembling stars.

My Life in the Movies

Opening scene: a bar in the old town. Dia framed by the open window as the sun sinks low, the fabric of a summer dress light upon her thighs. She raises a glass of cold white wine to her lips. We've drunk one jug and I'm about to fetch a second. But she remembers the dog. The husband's dog. Down one husband but stuck with the animal, incarcerated at home, gnawing the furniture. Gallant wave of my hand as she reaches for her money. And then she's gone.

Ritzi had watched it from behind the bar. He shrugged. With his eyes he offered his condolences, one guy to another. I sat with the empty glasses and watched the people in the street for a bit then got up and went to the urinals and read the old graffiti. When I came out I took a stool at the bar. Ritzi planted a fresh jug of wine on the counter.

'Hey, Ritzi, why don't you put some soap back there?'

'Why don't you, comrade?'

Soon he'd have me scrubbing the stalls. I wasn't paying for the wine. I was between jobs and slept on his floor. His couch was too short to lie on.

I continued drinking, my back to the world. Outside the street was darkening and in the interior dimness a constellation of coloured lights rose among the bottles behind the bar. The talk was a level hum. Vague figures drifted about me. I put on my diving gear and went underwater. A kelp forest swayed gently in the heavy green swell. They could have rearranged the furniture and repainted the walls, I wouldn't have cared. When Ritzi clapped his hands in front of my face I broke the waves. Heard voices again.

'He saw your film,' said Ritzi, gesturing to one of the regulars at the far end of the bar. 'You never said it was out.'

Cut to three years before. Dia was doing her PhD in linguistics, Ritzi played bass in a band, now defunct, and a character called Emil had asked me to write a screenplay for his debut film.

Emil gave me gonorrhoea too, indirectly. I'd been in love with a girl called Monica, and then ensued a painful break-up, except for a series of drunken weekend fucks, each supposedly the last. I recall their erotic intensity and the brevity of the analgesic effect. Next thing I was down at the clinic, getting my urethra swabbed. The doctor then had me lie on my front and before I could ask what was happening he had the glove on and his middle finger up my hole.

Your inner life, with its excuses and alibis and deceptions, has a sweetly dreamlike flow. You notice that quality when the movement is arrested. When it's smeared across a slide and examined beneath a microscope and comes back labelled with a name from hell.

Before I could tell Moni, I had to see someone else. Iuliana was a first-year student. She'd come to the city to study literature and foreign languages, met a slightly interesting, slightly older man who was writing for the movies and now she had the clap. An education you can't get from books. She was penniless. The parents sent food packages with the drivers of provincial buses every two weeks. She shared a small bare room in a student dorm with three other girls.

We sat on the edge of her iron-frame bed, the little carton of antibiotics between us. Snow was falling heavily outside the window. She asked the name of my disease. Her mouth moved to repeat the word but no sound came. I saddened her further by saying she needed to talk with any other men she'd been with recently. But it was as I'd feared. Only the boyfriend in the village back in the season of fumbling adolescent love. And me.

She was pretty despite her goofy glasses. And of her firm teenage plumpness there was nothing not to like. I'd slap her rump just to make her squeal and see her wriggle across the sheets. She was serious and honest. Her grip was desperate when we fucked and I know she had her daydreams about me.

There is a very short story by Chekhov, probably an early one from his days studying medicine and trying to keep his chaotic family from starvation—his father was a drunkard and I think his older brother was dying of tuberculosis— by churning out sketches for the magazines. It's probably called 'A Joke' or 'A Sleigh Ride': The narrator toboggans down a steep slope with a girl. The speed terrifies her and she clasps him tightly as they hurtle down. The wind rushes in their ears. The world is a blur. And he whispers to her, as a joke: '*I love you!*'

They crash to a halt at the bottom. She looks at him,

her face flushed from the wind and the thrill of speed, for confirmation of what she has heard. But he acts as if nothing has happened.

So she insists they repeat the sleigh ride. And he repeats the joke. Maybe they do it a third time, or go on doing it all afternoon. I can't remember. She has to keep hearing those words she can't believe she's heard.

I walked away from the dorms, penitent, busted, leaving my footprints in the fresh snow.

But still a schemer. I was able to go straight to Moni and claim I'd been with no one but her.

So she told me about Emil. They had 'feelings'.

To this day I dislike the word.

I'd introduced them.

Makes you queasy when you leave the room and they shift the scenery. From male lead to supporting actor.

Ruddy-skinned, like a pantomime devil, with dark sparkling eyes and girlish lashes, and tending towards corpulence—I'd lacked the imagination to see him as a rival in love. And least of all for Moni, who was suddenly more dear to me than ever.

Moni went and talked to Emil, who swore he hadn't been with anybody else. Moni told me she believed him.

I saw how it would be, and said no more.

We all took our medicine.

I was unable to avoid Emil entirely, because of the screenplay I'd recently done for him. The money was imminent. We met in a bar a couple of days afterwards.

'What the hell, we catch colds off each other all the time and nobody makes a fuss,' he said, as we grabbed our beers from the bar.

'Who's making a fuss?'

We found seats at a table.

'It'll stop dripping soon enough,' he continued. 'Takes a few days for the tetracycline to kick in. Your first dose?'

'We don't need to talk about it.'

But talk I did, a couple of beers in. And when I imitated the voice of the very thorough medic asking how it felt as he palpated my prostate, Emil sprayed the table with beer. It came out his nose.

I met up with Moni again the day after I'd seen Emil. 'How could you sleep with that clown?' I asked, pained and exasperated and finally failing to be the cool cat I aspired to be.

'How can you talk about him that way?' she replied. 'He's your friend!'

Shortly after, she moved in with him.

I loved her, after she was gone, with that pure burning love that abandonment causes.

They've been together since.

A few months after that I met Carmen. Decided it was time to be a reliable sort of man. I had money then and had found a good apartment. Sure, I told her, we're crazy about each other, grab your stuff.

About a year later, with the film about to go into production and my little advance long spent, I asked Emil when the real money would appear.

We were trying out a new bar. A place called Letters. Awkward orange and yellow furniture. Angles and attitude. The writing on the wall in the form of senseless fragments of text in various fonts and sizes. Behind the bar, the sci-fi bling of a back-lit display of bottles of coloured liquors. Around us, the new species of male that was invading the planet—skinny, blow-dried, finicky about attire and grooming. Aliens, hunched into the screens of laptops and hand-held devices, attentive as lovers, faces palely illumined in the hypnotic masturbatory glow.

The beers, when they came, were small. But expensive, due to the technology invested in their shrinkage.

I asked Emil about the money. He frowned and took a swig, and in the ensuing pause I sensed something was not quite right.

'See, the investors grab it. We won't see a penny.'

Emil did everything on expenses. That was his scam. Living was free. While I was tied to a job, paying the rent by writing a TV soap called *Day After Day*.

I went home to Carmen that evening and she got on the phone to a lawyer-cousin who agreed to look at the contract. He was a divorce lawyer.

The following day I climbed the massive staircase to Cousin Victor's first-floor office. The secretary paged him and seconds later he strode out and shook my hand. A large man, almost handsome, black hair, longish on top, parted neatly and slicked back. He held his chin up, kissing the air, so you might not notice the onset of jowls. A soft-fabric shirt and a bright paisley tie—as if the lawyer-thing was a bit of a lark. He only lacked a carnation in his buttonhole. He conducted me to his office and we sat down. The secretary brought coffee on a silver tray. I drank it and looked at the framed ink sketches on the walls. Victor skim-read the contract, nodded, and handed the pages back to me.

'You've been rear-ended.'

I was at the back of the queue of people to be paid, he explained. I asked how he knew.

'The contract doesn't specify, so the other party has the wiggle.'

I muttered something about betrayal. I admired Emil. Ten years older than me, he had been around. He had encouraged my scribbles.

'That's business. At least you're not a couple. My friends joke that in this world of broken marriages I'm the only Victor.'

Later on, when I had become good friends with Victor, he confessed with a trace of embarrassment, as though he were being unfaithful to his profession, how he did his best to steer his wounded, raging clients from the path of vindictiveness.

There in his office that day, Cousin Victor told me, with a shy smile, hand lingering on his heart, or the silkiness of his tie, that in the evenings, having put aside the business of the day, he wrote stories and poems. I understood then why he was generously sharing his time. We were both artists.

I went home to Carmen and to my nice apartment. And continued writing *Day After Day*. It was a gig Emil, my benefactor, had got me. I'd meant it to be temporary but it went on for years. Until I quit, and quit Carmen and my nice apartment, and ended up on Ritzi's floor.

The film came out. One afternoon I slouched down at the back of one of the last of the old cinemas not driven out of business by the multiplexes. Five or six pensioners in dishevelled grey clothing shuffled in like ghosts, and there were a couple of girls, probably students, whispering and nibbling sunflower seeds, gathering the husks on a napkin on the armrest between them. Ninety minutes later the credits rolled and I joined the drift, head down, back to the glaring street. My expectations had been low, but not nearly low enough.

I'd avoided Emil for two years, since the thing about money, and skipped the premiere, but now I wanted to see him. We talked on the phone and he invited me to his new home. Turned out to be the top of a glassy tower, a successful zoning violation with a view over a part of town where the other buildings are old and stunted. Moni was not at home. I hadn't seen her in a long time either. Emil put a bottle in a bucket of ice and I followed him up a spiral staircase to his rooftop terrace.

He filled our glasses. I can't say the city glittered but the lights were interesting and we were above it all. I leaned against the parapet and drank the clear cold wine and told him about leaving Carmen and quitting *Day After Day*. Everybody had slept with everybody, I told him, and every secret had been exposed. Never mind, he said, there's another movie on the way, the money's in the bank, and I'd like you to work on the screenplay. I made a face when he said the name of the financer—a well-connected ex-gangster. Well, said Emil, *pecunia non olet*, and anyway, if shit smelled like roses, then when we sniffed a bouquet we'd say roses smelled like shit. He told a tale of his days of vagabondage in the previous century, hanging around the Münchener Hauptbahnhof, needing to take a dump but not wanting to part with the fee. He reconnoitred the station environs for an alley or a bit of wasteland, like at home, where you might improvise, but every bit of space was utilised. Icy gusts from the north sliced his clothes and stung his eyes. He returned to the toilets in the station. 'I sat there, trousers round my ankles. It was wonderfully clean and quiet. And warm! I was worn out from travel, hadn't seen a bed in days. I dozed off at one point. I spent most of the morning there and nobody bothered me. I sat on my little throne, thinking about life, feeling safe. There was a background odour like they'd put a little pot of turds on to simmer, but I didn't mind. And ever since, the smell of warm shit and cheap disinfectant takes me back to it, like a Proustian fairy-cake.'

Something about the cool breeze and the wine and the weak sparkle of the untidy life of the poor streets beneath us tricked me into believing Emil knew something I didn't, and I forgot to tell him what I thought of our cinematic failure—which was my reason for going to see him in the first place.

An idea had been buzzing in my skull in the underwater hours after Dia scarpered. It had to do with the dog. And a conversation I'd had with her husband, Alex, about how he tormented it, imprisoning it in his little apartment. I don't like dogs and I don't care for people who like dogs. I can nearly understand people who like their kids, you get attached to them. But to make the decision to share your small apartment with a dog? Alex was an old pal of mine but by that stage I found his choked existence distasteful. It resembled his dog's, and my own slow suffocation, so I was talking about myself really as I riffed on canine abuse. I split up with Carmen the next day. A long time coming, but sudden all the same. About then Alex flew off too, went to Italy, and that was good, because I liked his wife, as Carmen had rightly intuited, and then I saw Dia in the street and called out her name through a big open window.

So, my old betrayer Emil let me sniff his money and then I went and slept on Ritzi's floorboards and the next day rose and bought a notepad and pen and some soap. Ritzi was sleepy and drinking coffee when I entered the bar. He opened the door at an indeterminate time in the afternoon but for the first hour or so might still tell any stranger who entered he was closed. He nodded and poured me a jug of red. I was coming and going with enough regularity that it was not necessary to speak. I unwrapped the bar of soap and put it on the sink in the bathroom. Then I took the table by the window and wrote by natural light and drank the wine.

I wrote that second screenplay when I was practically living in Ritzi's bar.

I'd go there in the afternoons and watch the street and write until the bar was too full and I was too drunk. It was a low time. I was broke and I'd unstick my cheek from Ritzi's floorboards towards midday. But it was a high time too, with a feeling that everything was in pieces, floating far too freely; you had to grab whatever came your way, and keep drinking to keep surfing an emotional surge that resembled the summer you were nineteen and on the brink of the revelation of your future self. I knew this fragile alcoholic mood was liable to flip like April weather or collapse in exhaustion, and that made it urgent. Then one night Dia was there too. She'd joined the party.

You know what happens when you fall in love?

You think you can see the future.

And maybe you can. Just a little bit.

That was last summer. I don't sleep on Ritzi's floor anymore. Ritzi's met a punky-looking girl who plays classical violoncello and they're talking about going to Brazil together. I have a small, rented apartment of my own now. Emil is making the film. He's hinted at an entanglement with the female lead. I'd lay money on this preceding her landing the part. He's talking about getting married too. Moni is pregnant. He tells me he thinks he'll be a great father. Maybe he will be.

I played him at tennis recently, for the first time in years. He's the better player, but I expected his weight gain in the interval to work in my favour if I could make him run a bit. He strutted onto the court in his whites, performed stretching exercises, huffing and grunting clownishly, and dispatched me in three straight sets. With deft flicks of his racket he ran me around the court. Sweat was in my eyes. I grew angry. Too eager to win points, I kept smashing the ball out of play.

He is destroying my screenplay. Injecting drama, giving it what he calls depth. He thinks not enough happens in my version.

He told me of the changes he's making after our game of tennis. I stared at the dry clay by the net. I heard the balls being smacked back and forth on the other courts.

I did not get angry. I just nodded.

I've made good money on this one, in advance. Victor assisted me with the contract. 'The pre-nuptial,' as he called it.

I'm finished with these scenes, these characters. No more movies. There is surely a better way to make a living.

Meanwhile, there's a roof over my head and food in the fridge.

I go to the supermarket to pick up some things. I get bread and ice-cream, cheese and wine, olives and apples, peppers and fish. The churches are falling into ruin and one day the gleaming supermarkets will give us the peace we seek. The bounty of the earth will be arrayed there and we will receive it graciously. But not today, and not in this town. In the past, people wore themselves out in the fields beneath a burning sun, and now they do it where the food is already sliced and packaged. Long checkout lines snake back between the crowded, narrow aisles. Time slows down, and if you have a bad job, a back problem or an unhappy marriage you might regret attending this show.

Back outside, the traffic at the intersection is already snarled up. Trapped in their metal machines, the workers of the city are trying to get home, each an obstacle to all the others.

I cross the lanes of congealed traffic and turn into my street, leaving behind the rush-hour scream.

As I turn the key in the lock of my door I hear the impatient clatter of claws on the parquet. Miki comes to greet me and I lean over and let him lick me. Miki always gets to me before Dia does. She appears from the kitchen this time.

'Don't let him do that. No, don't try and kiss me. Go wash your face.'

I do what I'm told.

'Did you remember to buy peppers?'

I tell her I have peppers and wine and loaves and fishes and chocolate ice-cream. She's just in from work and Miki is leaping and slobbering in the space between us.

'I'd better walk the beast.'

Out we go. He strains on the lead, pulling me forward.

I had thought once that man domesticated the dog and kept him prisoner, but I know the creature better now and I have a vision of him in the dark prehistoric night, the smoke and burning meat from the campfire in his nostrils, learning to be sneaky and ingratiating. Miki knows how to act friendly or submissive, how to look sad. He was there when the man first slapped his painted palm on the cave wall and declared himself an artist.

And so he walks me around the block.

Tree trunks and lamp posts. They all belong to him. He sniffs intensively, and lifts a leg.

I was walking him in the park last week and had just gathered his warm turds in a black plastic bag and was looking for a bin and checking out a lean pony-tailed young runner when she smiled and jogged up to me. Iuliana, without the glasses. She did a few stretches and told me she had a scholarship, was headed for New York. I told her something about my life in the movies. She looked taller than before, or I felt shorter, and I remembered I'd known her only in winter, and the strangeness of meeting this version of my former lover among the summer trees made me think I should have been with her, could have been, that I have no idea what I'm doing, that all I do is figure out some kind of a story to tell myself afterwards, but then she was wishing me luck and was jogging away and I still had that little plastic bag to get rid of.

I get back to the apartment and let Miki off the leash. He settles in the corner. Dia is cutting peppers in the kitchen. I take the wine from the fridge and open it and pour us each a glass.

I take my glass and go and sit on the balcony and have a drink and look over the city.

The crows begin their evening return to wherever it is they go. Along their journey they settle in clusters on the roofs and in the branches and on the wires, and then they panic, again in groups, and move on, becoming steadily more unsettled and dispersed as the sunlight weakens.

She calls me. Dinner is ready. I get up and go join her at the table.

Our kitchen is small but filled with the last of the evening light. I sit down opposite her. And I wonder why I seem to observe these scenes from outside, unsure what will happen next, and pretending I feel no confusion.

She smiles at me, lovingly, as though I am a three-dimensional man. I feel vaguely ashamed in her presence.

London

He laced up his boots slowly and put on his coat. He took the leash from the hook by the front door and shouted across the living room towards the kitchen doorway:

—Taking London round the block.

He could not see his wife from where he stood. She was sitting at the kitchen table with her laptop, and did not answer immediately. The kids were colouring with crayons, kneeling before a blocky wooden coffee table, and did not look up at him when he spoke. The boy was five years old and the girl was three. The boy was fair and blue-eyed like his mother and the girl had her father's dark eyes. Okay, said his wife, and he heard her chair move, then saw her backlit shape glide past the open kitchen doorway. The kitchen tap ran, briefly, then her silhouette passed again before the doorway, carrying a glass of water, and she resumed her seat. It was one of those moments, rare enough, when no television or radio played, when there was no music, no agitated voices from the screen, and when the day's work was done and they were all gathered in.

He stepped outside. With his own hands he had built the open wooden porch that ran along the front of the house. His wife had not been sure that such a porch would suit the house. It was a city house, built of brick and plaster some eighty years before, and when he showed her the plans she had misgivings. His American movie-porch, she called it. He admitted he probably liked the idea because it reminded him of something he had seen in a film, suggested another life. But when it was done she agreed that its proportions, at least, suited the building. He especially liked on bright summer mornings to open the door and step out barefoot, to feel the wood beneath his feet. He would stand there, clasping a mug of coffee, as the sunlight shone through the broad translucent green leaves of the walnut tree. A swing hung from its broadest bough. It was not country life but it was not bad either.

In their first years together, they had lived in one of those apartment blocks where you heard when the neighbour above flushed the toilet and the neighbours below quarrelled or made up. Then the children came along and they found they could afford to move to a quiet residential street in an old area not far from the centre of the city. They had their own entrance to their own house with a patch of gravel to park the car and even a small yard with a giant walnut tree. The first thing he did, before attempting the repairs and improvements needed—there were many— was to put up a children's swing in the walnut tree.

They worked hard. Both of them. And they were usually tired. And the children woke at night, screaming, needing feeding, or because they were teething, and later again having nightmares they still did not have the words to describe. But the man was grateful. It was the way life was supposed to be, he knew, though the peace and goodness also created dangers he had never previously known. The world was full of objects his children would fall and cut themselves on. Every time you turned on the television there were reports of cruelties inflicted upon the innocent and of freakish mortal accidents. When his first child was born and he had held him in his arms he had learned what his own strength was for. The lesson was that strength existed to protect the defenceless. It was a simple trick nature played on the strong, who one day open their eyes and find they are the servants of the weak.

He walked across the yard to where the dog was chained. The first smell of winter was in the air. Perhaps it was a taste of smoke. He did not know. The sky was banded grey above the darkening rooftops. With the fading light of the season, the living room windows glowed with soft red lamplight when he looked back at the house. The dog stood up to meet him when he approached.

—Hey, London.

A placid creature, but the jaws were made to crack bones. It had the massive head and neck of a wolf. When they had taken London in, back at the height of the summer, he had discussed with his wife whether wolves and dogs could interbreed. He was certain they were separate species. Dogs, he explained, were creatures that in prehistory slunk ever closer to the campfires of human settlements, preferring to scavenge rather than to hunt. Wolves kept their distance from human things. While he expressed these and other intuitions she typed keywords into her smartphone and the information came back directly that dogs and wolves could in fact interbreed. The canine continuum, she called it.

He undid the chain and caressed the dog. He clipped the

leash to the broad leather collar and immediately they were off, through the gate and down the street, the lead taut as the dog set the pace. Down one street then another, past all the houses, past households mysterious behind their fences and walls, past the parked cars, until they reached the silent church with the tall poplars dropping their last spinning leaves to the ground. The air was windless. It was a peaceful time in the life of the world. There were no riots, no armies advancing on the city, no plagues. All you had to do was wash the dishes after dinner and in the evening lay your head on the pillows of your marital bed.

It was nearly dark that summer evening several months before, when London found him. Swallows were flitting in the last light of a late summer sky and the trees stretched upwards in the warm air. His aimless stroll took him past the doorway of a little shop. Two men occupied the footpath outside, sitting on upturned beer crates, shirts unbuttoned, rolling dice across a backgammon board set upon a crate between them. It was a place where the locals sometimes congregated to talk and drink bottles of beer. He stepped into the roadway to pass by the players. It was at that moment he felt something tug at his hand.

He would later wonder that he felt no fright at feeling his hand gripped by the dog's teeth, or that the creature had slipped up behind him, silently, and showed no sign of releasing him, even as he continued walking. Though the dog's teeth were capable of inflicting damage, and he was a big animal—he presumed him to be male—he was holding the man's hand gently in his jaws.

He stopped walking, and the dog stopped too and

released his hand. They stood there in the darkening and deserted street. There was no sign of an owner. The dog had no collar. Its neck was huge and shaggy, the head too big. But the creature appeared pacific, perhaps even trained, and regarded the man tranquilly. One of its eyes was pale blue, almost white, as though damaged.

The man shrugged and continued walking and once again the dog caught up with him and took his hand gently with its teeth and walked alongside him. The streetlights came on, glowing orange against the indigo sky.

At several points on the walk home the man stopped and the dog would release his hand. He said things like, Go on boy, get lost. When he reached his gate, he had to let the dog accompany him into the yard. Once inside the gate, the dog walked over to the walnut tree—the swing hanging from its broadest bough—and lay down at the base of the trunk, its head on its front paws. The open doors and windows of the house, through the screens he had recently put up against the mosquitoes, glowed with hazy light, and as he approached the doorway the distinctive smell of roasted peppers grew stronger. He ascended the three steps and passed through the screen door, looking back at the dog, who now made no attempt to follow him. In the living room the children were watching a film with talking cartoon animals. They were sitting on the ground on cushions, too close to the screen for their own good, and did not look up at him as he passed. In the kitchen his wife was sprinkling on the roasted and peeled peppers a vinaigrette he liked, made with crushed garlic and cumin. Condensation had formed on the bottle of white wine she had left on the table for him to open. The table was set with placemats and knives and forks. Bread had been put out, and cheese, and a tomato salad and olives. A light summer meal. The candle had not yet been lit. He washed his hands at the kitchen sink. Marks from the gentle but steady pressure of the dog's teeth were imprinted in his flesh.

—A dog followed me home. Come see.

She wiped her hands and followed him outside. After the brightness of the house the yard was darker than before and the dog, lying under the tree, was a shadow. She shook her head.

—It's ferocious. Look at the size of it.

He described to her the strange way the creature had escorted him home.

—Looks like he's here to stay, he said.

—I'm not having a dog like that around small children.

—Perhaps he used to live here.

—He followed you. He didn't lead you.

—He is beautiful though, you have to admit.

—I don't trust him. And look at his eyes.

The difference between the eyes could clearly be seen even in the fading light.

They went back into the house. He lit the candle. They ate their meal and afterwards put the children to bed. Then he filled a plastic bowl with water and brought it outside to the dog. The dog lapped at it thirstily.

As they lay in bed that night he thought about the strange dog, in the yard outside. It was a warm night. He would happily have slept outside too, on the wooden porch he had built. All he needed to do was to rig up a mosquito net. But he would have had to explain himself to the woman and it would no longer have been worth it. It was like that with many things. She was turning the pages of a book.

—He's gentle. He's used to people. But I'll get a collar and put him on a chain tomorrow.

—We can't keep him.

—I know. White Fang. That's a good name for him. The wolf in the Jack London story.

They argued about whether there was a story called 'White Fang' or if White Fang was the name of the domesticated wolf in the story called 'The Call of the Wild'. Different stories by Jack London were mixed in his memory. About a wolf becoming domesticated, about a husky joining a pack of wolves. It had been a long time since he had read them. She had forgotten her phone downstairs and suggested he fetch it so they could google White Fang. Forget it, he said.

When he woke the next morning he immediately rose and went to the window to assure himself that the dog had not disappeared during the night. He was still lying under the tree, head resting on his front paws.

—What will we do? he asked his wife, when she woke. I can put him out, but I think he'll just hang around outside the gate.

—Get a chain, she replied.

That evening after work he spent some time looking for a good thick collar to buy, the biggest he could find, and a long heavy chain. The dog let itself be chained up and the kids were warned to keep out of range because with a dog like that you never knew. And no owner turned up and in time they got used to the dog, and it was safe around the children, and it seemed a crazy thing to call it White Fang so instead they called it Jack London. Sometimes they called him Jack, but London was what finally stuck. And they found out that the pale eye—blue like a husky's—could see. And the eyes too, with time, began to seem less unsettling and the woman contained her suspicion.

He sat on a bench beside the church, beneath the poplars, and pulled a small bottle from his coat pocket and unscrewed the cap and drank it down. He put the empty bottle on the ground beneath the bench then unclipped London's chain from his collar. London became another creature. One that sprang through the air, twisting like a giant cat, elastic and electric and light. He pounced on leaves and ran in circles. The circles expanded and London ran around the church three times, blurring in the receding light. The man pulled his coat around him and his hood low over his eyes and lay down on the wooden bench, hands tucked under his armpits, and closed his eyes. He listened to the rhythm of London's feet.

London is gone. Around the corner, down another street, with the effortless velocity earthbound creatures possess only in dreams, rocketing then through the bigger streets, past pedestrians and parked cars. The sure beat carries him through gaps between moving vehicles, diagonally across a patch of grassy wasteland, and back to a busy street laced with tramlines. He runs between the twin gleaming magic rails, then is a curving arrow, a blur, shooting an intersection. Now he is catching up on the clunking swaying tram ahead, the amazed faces of standing passengers—children, mothers, pensioners—gaping out the rear window. The crawling boxed-in city has seen nothing like this. And now he has taken the outside lane, accelerating, beating traffic obedient to lights and rules, now turning sharply and shooting down a narrow alley between tall apartment blocks that cram out the sky. Up a set of steps as a puffing blowing middle-aged woman with a bag of purchases yanks open the door to her building. London cuts past and though his pelt hardly brushes her she totters and is left sitting on the ground, pop-eyed, mouth agape, oranges spilling down the steps. London takes the stairway with two bounds per flight, all the way to the fifth. He is on his hind legs, tall as a man now, scraping at the door. He tumbles forward as she opens up, shrieking with laughter, dressed in a red bathrobe, hair falling in her face. Nobody invited you in, she says, turning her back, stubbing out her cigarette. Normally she likes to flick them from the balcony, particularly at night when they become shooting stars. She drinks her drinks unmixed. She is not tall or slim but she knows that what happens when she lies on her belly and lifts her hips just a little is something that some of the great artists would have liked to witness, for the sake of their work, and she looks back and shows her teeth when she does it. Already he is leaping about her living room, kangaroo hops included, pink tongue lolling, getting scratches on her parquet and slobber on her coffee table photo volume on the limestone turrets of Anatolia. His tail sweeps from a lower bookshelf to the floor a row of shells collected from a beach in Lesbos. Whoah, boy! she says, advancing towards him, arms outspread, with great rocking hips, as the jazz xylophonist on her sound system climbs the slippy steps of his gay plinking keyboard north. Postcards and pictures decorate her walls. She knows the power of planed and varnished timber. She has her rugs and drapes and fabrics. There are sticky salty red fish eggs in her fridge and she loves them smeared on thickly buttered bread. She falls to her knees on a sheepskin rug, grabbing his shaggy neck behind the ears to tame his acrobatics. Down, boy! He licks her face and neck, nuzzles the seaweed perfume of her black-stubbled armpits. This is a surprise! she says. He barks a musket blast that double-booms between the white walls. On those walls are hung black-framed photographs of black things in snow. She falls back and her robe falls open and her lolling paps relax out sideways. His hand grips her hair and gives it a twist, enough to take back her head, for his teeth to get at her exposed neck.

He climbs off her and has a good look around. The bathwater is running. Something approaching peace is in the air. Were he totally drunk on clear alcohol at 4 a.m. with the rain pattering on the bones of the dead city laid out beneath the window he would think of staying.

He eases himself into the foamy water of the big tub, his arms hanging over the side. She enters then, broad hipped and swaying, steps into the water, facing him, smiling, one foot then the other, great bell-jugs swinging, the waves sloshing towards him and to the floor as she settles in. Obscenely intimate, she leans forward and lathers his matted hairy chest. One eye is pale and diseased but she does not seem to care. Time is passing. He feels a pain in his jaw, an intolerable constriction in this hot watery tub. He rages against her presumption. She covers her face against tidal waves of splashing suds as he rises, roaring. She hears slaps of bare feet against the tiled floor, claws clattering against the parquet.

Wait! she cries.

He is already gone.

The part of the planet he called home was tilting further from the sun, turning its face away, and the days of stretching out on the planks of the churchyard bench were coming to an end. He had dozed off. His feet were cold and the joints of his knees had stiffened with the chill. His mouth felt sticky-sour. He saw images of black objects against snow and opened his eyes when he heard the beat of London's feet. He sat up and saw the creature as it returned through the gates, slowing now for the final circuits of the church, three times. He admired its sleek muscularity, the clean markings about its head, the paler fur on its underside, the awful whiteness of the teeth. He petted the head and neck as the dog wound down, readied himself for the end. Good boy, London. The clipping of the chain, the acceptance of the master's leash. He patted the creature. Such a fine animal, even the blue eye as though by wise design.

He stood up, a little stiff from having lain in the cold. His left knee gave him some trouble when damp weather was coming, the result of an injury he could not even recall, and he felt it now, for the first few steps. London was subdued after his run. His nose was closer to the ground. The man took a pack of mints from his coat pocket and popped one into his mouth.

The sky above still held much light but earthwards, through the gathering valley-darkness of the buildings and trees, amber light shone from the windows of the houses and when he saw the lights of his own home it made him want to approach slowly, reverently. Jack London too was unwinding and coming to a stop. He opened the gate to his home and the dog slunk in ahead of him, into the yard, a shadow in the twilight. He loped forward slowly to where the end of his chain lay, and the man replayed the tender routine of patting his neck as he clipped him back in. London did not ever seem to mind being chained. Sometimes though the man observed the sleeping dog's legs twitching as it ran across fields in its dreams. In the street, a passing car broadcast music that shook the ground in bass shudders and rattled the windows of the house. The obscene sound retreated and then was entirely gone. Kids taking their hearts down to the mall, or around in circles. He missed none of it. They could keep their narcotic heartbreak. His was the right age to be, with the little throb in his left knee and sometimes nights when it was impossible to sleep, not from any great trouble but simply from the wonder of all that had fallen into his hands, and he asked himself on those nights, with the moon and the stars shining through the branches outside his little window and the woman fast asleep, if he was just the stunned spectator he sometimes guessed he was, or the bearer and guardian of a deep intuitive knowledge and he only had to believe it for it to be true. He remained like that for a minute, hunkered down, holding London by the collar, turning it slowly around in his mind, before he rose and went to the house.

In the little entrance hall he hung his coat and the leash. The time of the year was beginning when you did not linger in the streets. Returning, you felt the soft warmth when you closed the door behind you. The kids came running to him as he removed his boots. He went with them and admired the pictures they had drawn, and in the kitchen he kissed their mother, who was preparing pasta shells with ricotta and spinach and chopped walnuts from their tree and told him that his week for cooking began the next day, and he nodded and said he knew that. And they ate together, and had a conversation with the blue-eyed boy and the dark-eyed girl about the coldest place in the world, and the biggest ocean, and the highest mountain and would Jack London be cold when the snow came? He told them Jack London would be happy in the winter because he already wore a fur coat. The plates were cleared and the children were bathed and told stories by lamplight and kissed and put to bed. Then the television flickered for a while, pages were turned, she yawned, she climbed the stairs, he watched her feet disappear. And then the house was quiet and he could hear her moving around upstairs and from time to time an occasional vehicle passing on the road outside.

Then it got very quiet, the way he liked it. When the hum from the fridge in the kitchen ceased—he hadn't noticed it until then—it was quieter still. He heard a creak from upstairs as she turned in the bed. The breeze shushed through the branches of the walnut tree, where the leaves were becoming brittle and falling, and he imagined he heard the clink of Jack London's chain as the beast shifted in the night, and he thought of the way dogs describe little circles on the spot as they lie down, little corkscrews downwards to the earth. A little turn to spread the long grass flat, or to make a hollow in the snow, their bodies even in the long centuries of domesticity remembering the grass and the snow.

Deadbeat

I wake up crying—I know not why.

That said, I feel okay, this bright new morning in my seventh decade. And why not take a gulp of air and howl? Is it not how we greet the world at birth?

I sit at the edge of the bed, waiting for it to end. A pale brown dove is perched outside my window. He cocks his head and snaps my distress with the shutter of a black eye then shakes his feathers and flaps away. Eight storeys below, in the concrete valley of my street, a Gypsy is yodelling for scrap metal. I hear a slowly moving car toot its horn, the leisurely hammering of nails from a rooftop, and birds twittering in the trees. All these sounds, and others, come gently through the morning, through my weeping.

I brush my teeth and sob at the gallery of pictures the mental machine throws up—landscapes and people and fragments of conversation. I rinse and put away the toothbrush and observe myself at the act of crying, its gestural aspects, and shake my head at the stricken man in the glass.

In the kitchen, I weep into my coffee, and slurp and spill. I abandon the idea of eggs. I light a cigarette but the snivelling spoils the pleasure of the smoke. I stub it out and stare into the empty cup. The glad tiredness when tears subside—that childhood reward after the body shakes you like a rag—does not come.

I press the handkerchief to my face and go forth into the bright morning, to hit the street briskly. But right outside my apartment block my geriatric neighbour—he's even older than me—is bending over, wide rump splitting the rear pleat of his jacket as he tickles the ribs of a little mongrel stretched on its back, red tongue lolling. They must have sized each other up, this promiscuous pair, and said, Let's do it! The old boy straightens up, spectacle-lenses sheening beatifically, outsize dentures gleaming, as he tilts his horse-grin to the gods.

I hurry past, head down. To hear my laughter, you'd swear I was crazed with grief!

In the rushing boulevard the humans stomp past with their devices, ears plugged, declaiming aloud, addressing the air and gesturing, just as the insane used to do.

I slip into a side street, away from the mechanical din of the main drag of Stalinist blocks, and into a world of balconies and windows hit by sun. Arches and turrets and pillars, fairytale follies, scabby tangles of vines draping neglected façades. I dig this old stuff, the lightness of uncommunalised life and private gardens. A black-branched tree is strewn with white blooms, paradise of bees, ecstatic yacking birds above. I hurry past a billion exploding buds, seeking the cool green of the park.

In the playground, flurries of tiny humans whirl in currents and eddies, up and down the slide, around again, one after another. The insect reds and yellows and greens of their little outfits blur in my liquid vision. Retreating towards a secluded shady corner, head down, I pass a paunchy old clown sprawled on a sunlit bench. He wears tight black leather trousers with matching leather waistcoat and a bright red blazer with big silver buttons. He has one arm draped along the back of the bench, where his invisible lover sits. This sends my ribs spastic. I bite my lip, honk my shnozz, and shuffle past.

I reach the perfect bench, a little away from the main path, beneath whispering trees, and collapse there, panting, wobbly, sniffling—gently, gratefully—at this lovely world.

The passers-by have the decency to pretend I do not exist, except for one lady of mature years who slows her pace and cocks her head at me sympathetically. I bare my teeth at her like a crazed chimpanzee. Go get your own bananas, you old cunt!

The shade beneath the branches works its chilly magic. I peek out at the world, as from a cave, at the figures shifting in the nervous light. I succeed in settling. Perhaps I will light that cigarette now.

Then I catch sight of an ungraceful individual.

His right foot scuffs the dirt. Unsuitable footwear, perhaps, or an old injury. One of those troubled types who stare at the ground and fail to see it. Now I am slipping down a frozen slope, in slow motion, arrest myself with my fingernails, leaving little cartoon scratch marks on the ice.

I hunch over to hide my face with my handkerchief and gag myself, but I'm out of luck.

'Dad!'

He approaches in tender wonder.

'Allergic reaction!' I shout, honking into the wet rag.

He sits down, head tilted, and places a delicate hand on my shoulder. This would be comforting if he did not hate me. Goes back to when he was very small, me telling his mother I had become fixated on another female. She ran to the bathroom to puke. The porcelain gave her dry-heaves an operatic quality. The boy was on the floor, surrounded by coloured wooden blocks imprinted with chunky upper-case letters, gazing up at me questioningly, confused. The letter B was in his hand. A detail I would grimly recall in his adolescent years, when he never stopped calling me a bastard.

And now, seeing me bawling in a public garden, he lays aside the charge sheet. I tell him:

'Flowers. Pollen. Fizz-ee-o-logical!'

Awkward fumbling imitation of sobbing man pushing cigarette between lips, lighting up. Exhaling, resembles a locomotive chugging up a mountainside.

His fingers squeeze my shoulder. They dig in. He's sure the old carcass requires expurgation, that I am suffering a long-overdue breakdown. But try denying your tears—it only lends them poignancy. I remove his hand from my shoulder, as gently as I can. He looks into the distance and in the silence I feel the words assuming form and weight in his breast. It's driving me nuts.

'Listen, Dad,' he begins ponderously. 'Years have passed. Now that I'm bigger..."

Sobs of laughter! Bigger? This sack of waste is hitting forty! His teeth are rotting. See my dentist, I tell him, put it on my account. But he's afraid of pain. He's shrunk himself down, crawled into a mousehole, cowers from phantom catclaws!

'… I can see how a guy can fuck up. I know you're sorry. I'm sorry too, for the misunderstandings.'

Were it only so! A moment of clarity, bathing us in its light! To see the world washed of detritus, and to get away clean. This is how religions are born. I have another disastrous attempt on the cigarette. I cast it away. It smoulders profanely on the lettucy grass. In the cool humid shade I hear the chatter of the avian world. I clench my fists, groan between gritted teeth:

'And you listen to me! You can't spend your life belly-aching! You have to live!'

Fertile girls are walking past.

His mother was a pretty flower. I remember her stripped down to the last scraps of erotic nonsense, me abuzz at the maddening final obstacle.

And now this disoriented creature occupies the bench beside me.

'Dad! We have to get you to a doctor!'

Nothing will deter him from doing his duty to his deadbeat dad. The sooner he gets me to a doctor, the sooner I can shake him off.

He gravely shepherds me from the park and hails a cab. He gives the driver the name of the hospital. We are launched into the stream of traffic. The driver checks me out in the rear-view mirror. I grit my teeth against the sobs.

I've seen him skip from one crazy scheme to another, burning through his inheritance from his mother, racking up debts from banks and buddies, and getting bailed out by me. When a son asks for bread, says the Sermon on the Mount, what kind of dad deals him a stone? So I laid out the dough till there was no more. He's tied to me by anger. I've told him, it wasn't my fault your mother went nuts, she was that way when I met her.

Reality, of course, is unsatisfactory. We swivel our little heads about, looking for the culprit. Were I dead, would it help? There's always the universe, or God, or society to blame. But I'm still here, and this broken boy accumulates distress as he goes, and is always turning up at my door, exhibiting his sores, and hanging it all on me.

It's been a couple of years since I last set foot inside his apartment. The electricity company was threatening to cut the supply. It was a warm day but the windows were closed and the place stank. I was thirsty and asked for water. We went into the kitchen but he was unable to locate a glass. A ziggurat of dirty dishes rose from a sink of scummy grey water. Open cans and containers and the remains of take-out food littered the surfaces. On the ground he was losing space to incursions of empty bottles and plastic bags, general detritus and spillage. The bin was overflowing. All this though he never cooked—too much trouble. Forget the water, I told him. The fridge was an entire museum of neglected foodstuffs—mysterious jars, furry fruit, little cracked bricks of cheese. I didn't dare enter the bathroom. I followed him into his bedroom-living room. He had bundled his soiled laundry into a wardrobe but had been unable to get the door closed, and I found myself discussing the stock exchange. The previous year he had tapped me for investment capital to buy a computer system. He needed to monitor a number of screens simultaneously and these were now arrayed around a desk, flickering hypnotically in the dim room. He had a head for figures, and knew something about the markets. He'd been making money until a sulky gum-chewing Goth who called herself Electra descended on his life. Unfortunate moniker for a girl so low on sparkle. Infecta, I called her, privately—her black lipstick suggested a medieval plague. She hung about his place—she had no income—making giant, lumpy papier-mâché sculptures that when painted were the lurid guts of extraterrestrials that had crashed their spacecraft in the desert. When she departed to vandalise some other heart the boy lost interest in the material world and blew the pile on a couple of bad transactions. So there we were sitting about in the gloom in front of these diabolical glowing screens, the information stacked in twitching columns of dense hieroglyphs, and he needed me to pay the electric company to keep them alive and blinking, and to give him a little something extra besides so he could descend again into the underworld of the markets, to mine its magic seams. You've cleaned me out already, several times, I told him. What now, sell my furniture? I'm too old to sit cross-legged on a mat like a Jap.

He looked ashamed for a moment, then started wheedling for a smaller sum.

'Forget the stock exchange. Wash your dishes!'

'The sink is blocked.'

And he didn't have a plunger. He tapped one of the strings of twinkling data. He'd been watching it rise all day, he would have bought.

'How can you think about the markets, sitting in this stink? Sweep the floor! Take care of the little things. That's how we live. A little at a time. Look, your fingernails are dirty!'

He looked at his hands, startled by the evidence there. I seemed briefly to have broken through, to have reached him, but the moment of lucidity passed across his face as a flicker of anguish and he was a little boy again, when he would cry and I would hold his small body to ease his pain, and I felt a wave of sorrow for him, for his terrible weakness. Then, just as quickly, I turned furious at being a sucker for the old routine, furious at my own continued uselessness. The stench from the overflowing ashtrays on his work desk made me dizzy. The sun was going down and we were sitting in semi-darkness. Should I get up and turn on a light? Get up and leave? But I just sat there, dragged down into the entropic gloom. Over the never-washed windows hung ancient grey net curtains, left by a previous occupant. He needed to burn them. And to throw out the leftover construction materials and other junk that clogged the balcony, also dating from a previous stratum of habitation. There were even a couple of withered houseplants by the window. I could understand being negligent and letting a plant die. But to leave the desiccated evidence there for years, gathering dust? I wanted to pull his windows open to let in the air and the last of the day's natural light, and to say to him: Isn't that beautiful? Doesn't it give you a lift, to feel the breeze and see the world outside? These gifts are free, you know!

It was a father of idiot children who discovered the idea of God. He looked at them and a lightbulb came on. Aha, so that's how it works: God gives us all we need, and we rack our brains to figure out a way to shit on it.

I emptied my wallet in front of his screens and left, swearing I would not return.

The taxi pulls up in front of the hospital.

We enter the glossy lobby. The receptionist invites me to jump the queue and the people in line defer to my suffering. I'm not sure what kind of a doctor I need. I opt for a neurologist.

The boy sees me to the lift. This is it, I say. You've done your good deed, you can go now. I repeat this inside the lift, getting angrier, and at the door to the doctor's office. The doctor ushers me in, and the boy follows. As chief witness, and victim, he wishes to testify to the nature of my moral collapse. A courthouse would be better, with television cameras and reporters, but a judge of disease will do. You're making it worse, I snarl, and suddenly I feel I should have a walking stick, to raise aloft and shake in the air, as cracked old men do in times of crisis.

'We can't have this, I'm afraid,' says the doctor, quietly, but firmly. 'You'll have to wait outside.'

It soothes me to see the door shut on his face.

The doctor sits down, notes my personal details. He asks me what the trouble is 'today'. I explain.

'No physical pain whatsoever?'

'None. Laughing or getting angry, same deal. My chest shakes. Water comes out my eyes.'

'I see.'

He tests my reflexes, coordination, blood pressure. He writes something down. His face hardens. No symptoms of pathology. He does not like this nonsense.

'As you say, physiological. There are cases of fits of

hiccupping, sometimes going on for days. But crying is, whatever you say, something else. I'll have to recommend a psychological evaluation.'

'Inevitable, I suppose.'

I mean this to sound matter-of-fact but it escapes as a whimper. He writes down the details of the referral.

'Have you been under any particular strain?'

'Just the standard crap.'

'I'm going to prescribe a mild sedative to help your muscles relax and perhaps ease this... chronic... em...'

He looks over my shoulder, at the wall, as though it is written there.

'... Lachrymosity.'

He writes out the prescription, planting a noisy full stop after the name of the drug. He rips it from the pad and stands up and hands me the slip of paper.

'Come back to me in a day or two if there's no alleviation.'

'That's it?'

'Keep well hydrated.'

He smiles at me as we shake hands.

Out in the corridor, the boy jumps out of his seat. Tells the doctor I have a history of repressed emotion—soon he will say I pushed his mother into an early grave, that I am the source of the goaty stench at the bottom of creation. The doctor backs off, holding up his palms, brow wrinkling, already too close to the fumes—and shuts the door. It clicks gently.

We take the lift down. I sit in a corner while he gets my prescription filled. He returns with the little box of magic candy and an economy pack of menthol-scented paper handkerchiefs. He turns over the change—a few grubby coins—as though they were gold ducats. 'I'm tired,' I tell him. 'I need to lie down. To be alone.'

He follows me outside, insists he will take me home. This would be bearable, I feel, were it not for his clutching hands and the inability of my words to carry the simple messages I entrust them with.

Out in the street I punch the boy in the snout and he goes down.

It is not a hard punch. Neither well aimed nor premeditated. He is grasping at me and my arm jerks out to force him away. It is a glancing blow and I do not knock him down. It is more complicated. As I lash out he takes a half-step back off the kerb and his left foot goes from under him, twists, and he is falling back, flapping his arms as though trying to get airborne—no, swimming through the air, the backstroke perhaps. But he cannot fall, because a car is parked in the street, so now he is slipping down the side of the car.

It is all absurdly drawn out. I could take photographs of each stage and give them amusing titles. I could offer advice. No, don't put your foot there, you idiot! Put your right hand a little higher, to balance yourself! Once again, he is treating me to the spectacle of his collapse. I watch, horrified he will hurt himself, and at the same time repelled, and even suspect that this is the meaning of the whole thing, that this is what he wants—to fall so that I will pick him up.

A fat woman is standing with a child outside the clinic and she pulls the little girl to her. People in a slowing bus have witnessed it too. The vehicle has just pulled in a little ahead of us and is disgorging passengers. The boy is sprawled on the ground, shoulder half-wedged between the kerb and the wheel of the parked car, looking up at me, uncomprehending.

And I have seen exactly this look on his face before. I had taken him to a playground. He was five or six years old and mine for two Saturdays a month. A woman—not the one I had left his mother for, another one—was standing in the background, and I had put him on the roundabout. I spun the roundabout. Then I spun it faster and he flew off. And when I went over to him he was lying on his back, defeated, already too old to cry.

'You spinned me too fast!'

I picked him up and hugged him to me, and he refused to return my embrace.

'It's a roundabout. You're supposed to hold on!'

I had spun him and he had decided to release his grip. Is this what children do? Do you always have to remind them how to live?

I take advantage of him jammed down there and make a break for it. I hurry towards the rear exit of the bus, pushing past those who have just got out, make it on just before the automatic doors hiss and shut. A young woman slips out of her seat, deferring to my years. I slide into the seat and angle myself towards the window, clamping my teeth on my lower lip. I don't know where the bus is going. I will take it a few stops then disembark and make my way home. I pat my pocket, feel the medicine there.

We head towards the centre, along the little river pent between concrete banks like a giant open drain, to one side the palace of the dictator, vast and useless on its artificial hill, for which he bulldozed half a city—tens of thousands of homes smashed to rubble. The Holocaust monument comes into view and the strain of swallowing my tears makes me want to lay my lamentations there—but already the bus is rushing past, and not even a survivor of the camps would dump his grief before that shoddy lump of concrete, its red metal pillar jabbing heaven like a rusty chimney.

We shunt through the choked and angry heart of the city, its oriental confusions, its klaxon fanfare, its joyous screaming and swearing. The buildings rise higher into the air, the mess of signs and billboards gets more brash and insolent, and the people at ground level mill against each other and distress the frantic traffic by their periodic need to swarm the intersections. I watch the blind and hectic city with mounting horror as we jolt from cherry light to cherry light. Beggars board our swaying vessel and declaim by rote Homeric tales of severed limbs and fallen family pillars and broken walls and years of circuitous wandering. Outside, at the intersection, a pair of dogs copulate. A huddle of teenage boys—one holding the plastic cola bottle that is the nectar of sub-proletarian skank—shudder with idiot joy before this random casting of canine seed. This is the enactment of the scene of their own generation. As in the parable, some falls on rocks, some sprouts but withers beneath the burning sun or is choked by the weeds. And a few chance grains flourish to become rangy cornerboys, sideburns shaved to daggers, who sport tight white girly jeans cut to just below the knee and point-toed slip-on shoes of skin stripped from the underbelly of an albino crocodile. The bus rolls on through these streets, through the heart of the city and out the other side, into a strange neighbourhood of improvised and misconceived constructions. This is the general style of the town, just more so here, where less money drips down. Disregard for proportion or space, jostling pieces mismatched, new and old mixed together. Each building struggling to rise above its neighbour, like plants choked at the roots and burning themselves out in the hopeless dash towards the light.

The bus has emptied out. I am the final passenger when the driver cuts the engine. I disembark in a strange deserted street where pale dirt is thick on the ground and a man with his nose eaten away sits against the wall reciting a singsong halfwit poem. He might be begging or else his chant has turned inwards and become a prayer. Kids kick a half-deflated ball. I march the other way. A gust of wind kicks up dust. City filth long trapped beneath piles of ice, free at last. I don't know where I am. My condition is becoming chronic, but it seems that I have arrived in a place where nothing is remarkable and no one has any reason to be ashamed. Women with enormous hoop earrings, glinting silver wheels, step into the thoroughfare in pink or blue bathrobes and fluffy slippers, arms folded across their bosoms, others in apparel they have outgrown, brown breasts and haunches spilling out. Infants on their hips that could be their children or younger siblings. At sundown their brothers will be sidling out of alleyways, offering me a deal. I sight greenery at the end of the road, a hill, and press on, weeping, desperate for a secluded corner. A man seated on a step moans as I pass, and I see his drunken fingers working at one of the hospital bags that nourish or drain the body, the tube snaking into his tracksuit trousers. A trickle of liquid runs from the step towards the gutter and I do not know if his distress is at having slopped his can of beer or pissed himself. This side of town is two hops from my own but already the fabric is frayed and soiled. Here, the city surrenders its health. Nubile beauties wither beneath this dreadful sun. In these streets fertility is a transmissible disease. Its cracked footpaths are strewn with the limbless, the maimed, the defective, the palsied and crippled, and proud exhibitors of Talmudic skin diseases are its aristocracy. Is it the sudden good weather that brings the sick and the beggars out upon the street like cockroaches? In this carnival of dissolution there is an opportunistic attitude to decay and debility, that it might be worth a few coins, that a twisted broken limb is worth more than a healthy one. Civilisation—it dies from one side of town to another. Or from one generation to the next. Your power to communicate it may be lacking.

A procession is turning in from a sidestreet, clogging the road ahead. I rush forward to grab its tail, giddy at my luck. The bereaved lead the parade. At the rear are the bored and dutiful, footsore and dragged through the heat, but this will do, and I release my shuddering cries. I whoop it up at the back. Cancer? Heart attack? Suicide? Whatever moved you along, God bless and thanks, pal. We reach the greenery at the end of the street and tramp between spiked metal gates, guarded by a homeless man hanging on a cross.

'Get down off that thing, son!' I yelp, between sobs. 'You'll only get hurt!'

They plod glumly left, suffering beneath the sun, and I go straight. To find a cool place to rest, on my own, and wait for the spasms to recede. It is a low hill on the city's edge and I climb the broad path, wending upwards between the graves.

And now I am free to choose a comfortable spot among the fresh blooms and newly dead or the wild verdant tangle amidst the planted-long-ago, and release my tears, and not be shy.

I climb the hill, wheezing at my heart's enthusiasm, seeking the perfect point of rest, like an alcoholic plotting the day's first glass, and the city opens into view beneath me. An agglomeration of intentions and occurrences, no binding plan, no guiding principle, no law, all improvisation and furtive deals and dirty schemes, the grand vision fucked over by the sudden fix. I scramble into a side alley of the laid-to-rest, through overgrown trees and bushes and tilting stones, and dump myself in a bower overlooking the slope and the scattered dishevelled town beyond. I lay myself out, at last, beside my chosen stone, upon which is carved:

> *As you, knowing nothing,*
> *Give good gifts unto your children,*
> *The blessings of your father in heaven*
> *Are yours for the asking.*

The patient attention you give a child so it will grow strong. Is that the one sure gift? That even one such as me, knowing nothing, could have given? I wonder at the gifts I have distributed. They have not been the finest quality. I close my eyes and press my cheek against the cold rough stone and regard my remaining time.

Graceland

He bought the tickets and descended the marble stairway with his daughter. She was two years old and had to hang from his hand taking each of the big steps. She swung down with her right foot first, then with her left to the same level, over and over, until they reached the basement floor. Now they were underwater. Sharks and sturgeon and stingrays and carp and pike freeze-framed behind diorama glass. Something like sunlight flickered down through dark waves. They moved between the cases, still holding hands, and came to a beach, among seabirds and shore animals. They followed an estuary and river, crossed plains and woodland and ascended high into mountains inhabited by bear and goat and wild boar. Winter came, snow fell. A stag struggled against a pack of starving wolves. One wolf was on top of the stag, fangs locked on its shoulder. Another had fallen and was in mid-roll on its back in the snow. The stag tossed its giant antlers, with failing strength.

They moved across each continent, through prairie and desert and rainforest.

They came to a cave. At the entrance to the cave she stretched her arms towards him and he scooped her up and carried her in. Hidden speakers played an echoing soundtrack of drips and the squeaking of bats. They gripped each-other in the dimness, faces together, and he crept through the dark winding passage, past stalactites and stalagmites, through the danger.

They exited the cave and he set her down. They were in the arctic. Two adult polar bears and a cub stood on a rocky shore. Icebergs drifted in the background. She pointed at each animal in turn:

That's you. That's Mami. That's me.

He nodded.

They ascended a wide stairway, holding hands, to the middle level of the building. They saw skeletons of elephants and whales, then rocks and crystals of every colour pulled from the earth's depths, and garish cross-section models of the contents of a human cell, and giant pastel ladders of DNA that spiralled to the ceiling. A little further on, the Earth and Mars and Jupiter and Saturn and the moon and stars were projected onto the dome above their heads, and the birth of suns and black holes and the Big Bang was explained. They climbed a stairway to the upper level and life appeared on Earth. He picked up the little girl so she could put her hand in the mouth of a giant reptile. Then they crossed a gangway over an excavation where the bones of mastodon and mammoth and giant armadillo poked from the sandy ground. From that to lepidoptera of all sizes and shapes, papery wings spread and pinned, and their larvae and chrysalises. For a drum-roll finale, the beasts of the African savannah.

Then they were outside under the blue sky, in a city, with big roads to cross to get to the metro station. The world had stood still for them in the museum, but now it moved faster than ever.

Each time they went to the museum, she noticed new things and asked new questions. He lived it through her. But he was also outside it, prepared for accidents and delays. He carried a bag containing a snack, a small bottle of water, wet-wipes and some spare clothes. He knew when she had last eaten and what, and when she had last been to the toilet. His eye was always on the clock.

She sat on his knee on the metro home.

They emerged from the station beside the mall into the bright light of the middle of the day. He carried her on his shoulders. They went around the mall, along the main boulevard, and then through a gap between the cliff-face of apartment blocks and into their own street. It was an unbroken row of unpainted concrete buildings. The footpath one side of the street was entirely blocked with parked cars. The other side was free and lined with chestnut trees in full leaf. The sunlight through the leaves made them glow a mad lime-green. He stopped to let her pluck a leaf. She didn't have the strength, so he wrenched a bunch high on its stem and gave it to her. She carried the stem in her fist, the five big leaves spread like a fan before his face. He peeked out through the gaps.

Their journeys were always strewn with leaves, sticks, stones and flowers to be investigated and collected. She drew his gaze down into the detail and texture and colour of small things. They would discover a colony of ants and stoop to follow the line where it ascended a tree trunk or crossed a footpath and disappeared into a crack in the concrete. She registered birds and dogs and cats and an entire universe of living things that he would otherwise be deaf and blind to.

She saw monkeys too. There was an hour at dusk when she grew sleepy, before he put her to bed, when she stretched her arms upwards to him and he picked her up—such a little creature, so light and made to be held—and carried her down the stairs of the apartment block and outside into the prosaic streets of their concrete neighbourhood. They would go where the giant chestnuts grew and gaze upwards with craned necks at the lacing of black branches against the milky sky, looking for the monkeys that revealed themselves only at dusk. He would ask her to be very quiet and, their cheeks pressed together, he would point and whisper, Look!

And sometimes she could see them.

He opened the apartment door and stepped into the main room, which was kitchen and living room combined. The woman walked past him, towards the child's room. She saw him but did not speak. The little girl ran to join her. The apartment was dirty. He started to tidy and to clean. The woman was speaking to the girl in the adjoining room and he knew from her voice that something was not right. He had hoped that taking the child out of the apartment on a Saturday morning would allow her to rest and that she would be cheerful when they returned. Now he had the choice between asking her what was wrong or waiting in the hope that it would pass. It was hard to know which option would create less trouble. He opened the fridge to see what he could get the child for lunch and inside the fridge was filthy. He had put it off too long. He decided not to risk cleaning it while she was there. She would interpret it as a reproach. He would wait until she was out of the apartment. He took some eggs from the fridge to scramble. He opened a cupboard and got a bowl. The bowl made a sound as he placed it on the counter surface. He began cracking the eggs into the bowl.

An hour later, the eggs were still in the bowl, beaten, and she had left and taken the kid. While he had been out at the museum, she had opened a journal where he sometimes jotted stray thoughts and she had not liked them.

Indeed, he had written something. He had been in a hotel room on a bright day in early summer, some weeks before, in a provincial city, a Habsburg town of wide boulevards and leafy squares, with a park beside a broad river. Their room at the back of the big modern hotel had a view over the river and the park, and the linden trees were blooming. The kid had been left with the woman's parents, and they were alone together in a spacious room with a big bed with white sheets, and the green natural world was right outside the window. The far bank of the broad river was verdant too, and above the sky was blue. They had walked together through the town, down neglected sidestreets where the neoclassical façades crumbled, only minutes from the main boulevard along which ran old-fashioned trams with tinkling bells. They looked up at those windows and wondered at the grand rooms and airy ceilings. Later, when he had an hour of solitude, he opened his journal. He seldom wrote, from lack of time, but in the bright hours of that vast peaceful day he sat at the hotel-room desk and wrote about how only weeks before he had been afraid to take that trip with her to the provincial town. It had been a period when they had fought bitterly, and the exhaustion of it made him want to be alone. He wanted rest from the fighting. As it turned out, they did not fight on their trip and they were happy there together, and this was what he was thinking when he confessed his earlier misgivings to the empty pages.

What she understood from what she read was that he had not wanted her there. He tried to explain but the fight wore on and in the end the things he said made it worse and then she left.

He cooked the eggs and ate them. He wandered into the girl's room. The fan of chestnut leaves was on the parquet floor, wilted from the heat.

Hours passed. He dialled her number. She was at her sister's. She did not want to talk. Her parents were driving in from just outside the city to take the child away to their place.

Well now, he said, trying to keep his voice level and reasonable, she can stay with me in our own home. My child can stay with me. She doesn't have be sent away, out of the city. She told him coldly the arrangements had been made. He replied, careful to keep the fear from his voice, that they could be unmade. That conversation ended. Next he tried to call the grandparents but they did not answer. Phone to his ear, he visualised them tight-lipped and driving towards the city, the wheels of their vehicle spinning over the hot asphalt, seeing his number and letting it ring out. He tried calling them a second time, in vain. She had called ahead to warn them.

It was happening now, what he feared most. She was showing him how it would go for him. The features of the life he would inhabit were assuming shape. Like chess, down to a degrading scatter of pieces, playing a blocking game.

Was she so blinded that she could not know what she was doing? She was using the child. He was not sure this was something he would be able to forgive. He understood how men in such situations were capable of doing terrible, irrational things. He observed the desperation rising in himself. But now he needed to think more clearly and coldly than he had thought before. He hushed the violence. He whispered to it and caressed it like you would a cat to gain its trust then he gripped the loose skin of the nape and removed it squirming from the room. No, nothing unpleasant was going to happen.

The hours dragged in the childless apartment. Towards evening, as the sun dipped low, he took the short walk to his usual bar. It was a good bar. He could sit there at the counter and not talk to anybody and the girl behind the bar saw when his glass was empty. It was a place where he could think about things, looking at the wealth of coloured bottles in rows against the wall, the photographs and postcards and coloured banknotes. There were piles of books too, for decoration.

While he was thinking and looking at the bottles the bar filled up. People moved about, shouting and laughing, and the music got much louder. He ordered something small and drank it and then he felt like he was floating. He was suspicious for a moment of this sudden sense of being above the world, anaesthetised, then he just went with it. Elvis entered the building, followed by a Mexican outlaw with bandoliers and a beautiful girl in buckskins who was maybe Pocahontas. They moved to the back of the bar.

He turned to face the bottles again, and to think things through. The kid, when it was quiet, could hear and see things neither of her parents could. He lived through her. He remembered when she was smaller, sitting on her plastic high chair, him trying to get puréed food into her mouth without her making a mess or rubbing it in her hair—perhaps feeling that it was a task for someone who had slept or who did not have something more worthy to do—and how she sat up straight and said one of her first words. *Wuff! Wuff!* And then he would hear what she had heard and what he had been unable to register—a dog barking, two streets away, audible on a quiet Sunday when the machinery of the city had died down. How many other things was she hearing and seeing and smelling and tasting and finding extraordinary that he had become insensible to? Well, pretty much everything. It had something to do with time, he supposed, and reason, and planning. To achieve the objectives he had set himself—with this home, this situation with the woman, the need to care for the child and earn money so that their life in the city did not hopelessly unravel—his eyes saw beyond the horizon, towards something unreal.

Pocahontas appeared beside him, a long tanned arm extended, her hand on the bar. The long rope of her braid swayed. Her profile was very noble. He tried not to stare at the side of her face. He knew she forbade trivial conversation. She took the drinks and returned to Pancho Villa and The King.

Yes, he thought, contemplating the noble glowing rows of bottles, the real world was very far away and his senses were perverted. His ears were attuned to other sounds; the sounds of things being on course or about to spin off the rails. The sound of a dog barking on a clear quiet day did not penetrate it.

Sir?

Elvis was standing beside him, indicating the free barstool. He wore a white sequinned jumpsuit with a giant collar and a jewel-studded belt and purple-tinted sunglasses. He nodded to Elvis and Elvis sat down.

JB and Coke, said Elvis.

He observed Elvis receive his drink and noted that at the back of the bar Pancho and Pocahontas were becoming amorous. Elvis shrugged and took a pull at his tall glass.

Elvis had been the most beautiful man on Earth. Dreaming his own dream like Adam in the Garden, a King stumbling towards his Queen, a song upon his tongue, to make his kingdom complete.

She had taken the child and reduced the game to its barest elements and he hated her for that. But he would stay with the woman. He would be stronger than her, more silent, more restrained. He would be a piece of stone. Whatever she rained on his shoulders would wash off him. Then he heard his own voice, after he had spoken:

What happened back there? You were doing fine for a time.

Yessir. One year I was chosen one of the ten outstanding young men in America. It was a real honour for me. I was very proud.

Three movies a year. The actresses?

Not all the songs were good. I had to gear down to situations.

You were a hound dog, Elvis Aaron.

Uh huh.

He told Elvis his thoughts. He told him the little girl was hearing things, seeing things and touching the world for the very first time. And above her floated the voices of the parents—only intonations for now, that later would grow clear—dividing the realm. Sometimes Elvis nodded. Neither of them spoke for a time, then he said:

You're there, Elvis. You're in Vegas now. This is it.

For a moment Elvis seemed not to have heard, or was trying to remember something.

She's not going to take my kid, he told Elvis, decisively. She might as well try and kill me.

Sir, you're already dead, said Elvis, looking straight ahead, holding on to the bar with two hands and easing himself off the stool. You don't live in Graceland now. You're faking it.

The King was looking around as though waking and realising he was in the wrong place. He got out some money to pay the bar-girl, but grew confused by the different pieces of paper. He let her take what she needed.

Thank you. Thank you very much, said Elvis.

He lurched towards the door.

First Love

30 June 1941, Krakau

Sleepless nights. Yesterday I volunteered for an Operation. Today the order came. Within hours we were gone. Parting from Trude—terrible. I can make no sense of it.

Only last night, lying beside her, single candle burning, I sang the verse about our two shadows melding by the light of the barracks lantern as I yearned to stay and had to go. She laughed, said she never knew when I was joking. I was sincere, but when I sat up to pour some water from the carafe I caught my reflection in the mirror and in the flickering light could not believe myself. It was a movie scene. I could not trust anything I felt or said. Singing a sentimental tune to another man's fiancée. I was split in two. My old self sat in cold judgement, even as I hurled myself into the drama. I was mad with jealousy. A week of this kind of thing. It felt much longer.

Departure was delayed several times. At 1700 hours we finally left Radom. Then the dusty road, the countryside under the settling sun, the rows of poplars casting their shadows. The feeling of motion strengthened me, and in her absence it was clear. It was love. My first love. The other times are nothing beside it. It illuminates everything, and everything hangs on it, even now as the kilometres multiply and the distance between us grows.

Reached Krakau at 0230 hours. Our quarters are clean but we sleep on bare boards. I am exhausted yet feel I could write until dawn. I will command myself to stop. I will sleep as soon as I put my head down.

2 July, Millnicze

Passed through Przemśl, the front line, only days ago. Roadway littered with shot-up armour—bizarre Russian armoured cars, like jalopies topped with gun turrets. Towards Millnicze, dying horses, roadside graves of soldiers. Got here at sundown, quartered in Russian military school. By 2300 hours could finally retire. Inquired when letters could be sent—impossible for now. I write this instead. If I lie down the pen will slip from my fingers. The exhaustion, the road, the separation. I may never see her again.

Those nights of broken sleep, not knowing the hour, reaching out to see if she was still there. Moving in and out of dreams, the endless coupling in the dark, the sun rising again.

He could have burst through the door at any moment. Both of us with our pistols. Dangerous scene but ridiculous—cheap drama in a provincial theatre.

I would have despised myself had I not volunteered.

*

3 July, Lemberg

Woken by bugles at 0600 hours. The town still smouldering, women and children rummaging in ruined houses. Ukrainian soldiers, our new comrades. The smell of decomposing corpses, the roar of vehicles, the road running forever east, to Siberia, to the Pacific. Nervous peasants. Only the children dare meet your eye. Anybody over thirty has seen the armies of Franz Joseph and the Tsar, then Poles and Bolsheviks, back and forth.

Several evenings ago, on a porch, a sunset, our imminent parting, watchfully restraining the feeling in my voice as the sky darkened and the air cooled. A precarious light, a mood, a few tinkling notes at the end of a melody. Sky oozing colour like those Bosnian cakes drip syrup.

For the personal to assume such proportions now, when the world is being remade—madness.

Compared to Warschau, Lemberg is tranquil. Again quartered in a Bolshevik military school. Reds didn't know what hit them. Salvaged what we needed from what they left behind as the Jews scurried about, cleaning up. I have so many thoughts, impressions, but it is almost midnight and they're all for Trude. I speak to her in my head, constantly.

4 July

A chance mail will soon be sent. Writing my first, frenzied letter to her—sensual music on the radio—when the order came. Commando Operation—steel helmet, rifle, thirty rounds. Five hundred Jews lined up in a courtyard. In the end, the execution didn't take place, but we're still on standby. Earlier we were shown the bodies of murdered

German airmen and Ukrainians. The prison where they committed many of their atrocities is nailed shut. Not that I care for shooting unarmed prisoners. Even Jews and Bolsheviks. I prefer straight combat.

Rumour we're going back to Radom, another that we're going east. Reds retreating in disorder. Morale is good.

5 July

Before midday. Marvellous music on the radio: '*Hörst du mein heimliches Rufen?*'

A beautiful 21-year-old woman. So, she had her fun. I wondered how bad things could get for me. Well, I extricated myself. Left her to her fiancé.

Him at the front, doing his duty—this cast me in an ignoble light. But now I am doing my duty, unafraid of the road ahead. The battle is a fair one. I opened my heart to her in yesterday's letter. Told her I am hers. And so it is for her to decide.

If only I could see her.

Lemberg is not pacified. Fanatical Poles. Jewish commissars who have shrugged off their uniforms and mingled among the civilians. Wehrmacht sentry found shot a few streets from us before dawn. An hour later, at 0500 hours, thirty-two Poles from the resistance movement dug their own graves a few hundred metres from our quarters. One of them wouldn't die. Covered with sand, but a hand emerges, he's lifting himself up, pointing to his heart and saying, I suppose, Come on, do it right.

First hot meal today. Also, received 10 Reichsmark. Bought a whip for 2 RM.

Smell of corpses everywhere. Sleep when I can. Another three hundred Poles and Jews dispatched in the afternoon. Evening trip into town. We wanted to inspect a jail where the Bolsheviks had done their murdering but the stench hit you from streets away. Couldn't have entered the cellars without gas masks. Then, Jews tottering about at a street corner, covered in dirt. My first thought—this morning's group had crawled out of their graves. Questioned them; the Ukrainians had rounded up some eight hundred at the GPU building to shoot for involvement in Bolshevik terror, but they were being released. We drove towards the citadel. Hundreds of bloodied Jews. Some running away, others falling down to die. Gruesome scenes at the citadel, Jews running the gauntlet of soldiers lashing out with cudgels, bodies piling up, sometimes one of them rising, whimpering and stumbling away. We ask who's in charge. Nobody. The Jews are being let go, that's all, and the soldiers are angry, having seen the work done to their air-force comrades—fingernails extracted, ears cut off, eyes gouged. Even so, I disagree with this kind of public spectacle.

Such luxury to have the radio. Rich, sensual music. At any moment we could be packed off east. Tense mood among my comrades. We'd rather be closer to the action. This operation is disappointing. The lack of real combat is frustrating.

6 July

Bad dreams. Black depression. Sent another letter. I have made my declaration and can only repeat it. But I get no letters back, and the talking in my head, speaking to her, gets worse. I have to get to Radom. Failing that, only the road again, or hard combat, can relieve this pain. I should not have written to her today, in this mood. It was what I dreaded doing, what I despise—one step away from begging.

First time we made love, she had her period and she was ashamed afterwards. Alone in the bathroom, as the flowing water carried her blood from my skin, all I felt was tenderness. It was her precious red blood, the same as if she had cut her finger, and I rinsed it from me and went back to her. Nothing felt the same when I was with her. Nothing was ever ordinary. That tenderness remained even when I feared she was playing with me. Even when I was drunk I managed not to say cheap things to stab, to intentionally wound. Even now, I could not say a word to hurt her, though she has hurt me so badly.

7 July

Tomorrow, Commando Radom heads for an industrial town south of here, Drohobycz. Collective sigh of relief. The district is partly occupied by Russians and we will have the chance to make a difference, thank God. I will volunteer for the more dangerous tasks. Pockets of fanatics will present themselves behind our lines if they are not stamped out. I feel we have been here a year. Had time to scour the town for a stationery shop. Real writing paper does not exist here but I found some envelopes—had been scrounging from my comrades. Also, a big travel bag for 32 Rubles/3.80 RM. Tomorrow, mail going to Krakau and Lublin, from where it will be sent on.

Yesterday, news of the capitulation of another 52,000 Russians. Don't see how they can go on like this—there'll be revolution in Russia within weeks. Celebrated with our comrades from Krakau last night.

Drohobycz, 8 July

Set off at 0800 hours. Our luggage has increased with equipment and personal items salvaged from the Russians, though we've lost a couple of trucks to other units. Oberführer Schoenrad heads our Commando, Sturmbannführer Roeck heads the operation. Again, the stench from the jail many streets away. Crowds massing in front of every shop, hoping for food.

Arrived in Drohobycz at 1600 hours, occupied a hotel, then split up to scout for more long-term quarters. Former apartments of communist functionaries, decent bathrooms. The Ukrainians have done a good job looting. Thought they were going to be in charge. That will be clarified for them shortly. For now, lodgings are modest. I 'inspected' the kitchen, got something for my belly. Insects everywhere.

Feel we'll be in this town for some time—weeks or months. We're certainly not going back to Radom.

I've sent letters but nothing back. Has she received them? Has she written? Is there a letter for me now in Lemberg? It's infuriating. Must finish this. I have sentry duty until the morning.

*

9 July

Our new HQ—former communist party army school. I'm in charge of equestrian matters already and have got hold of several ponies. Seems I will have something to do with economic organisation also.

Coming off sentry duty, three slatterns ambush me—hotel 'maids'. Don't know if this was a brothel or they're just hungry. Evening—party with my comrades, dinner, very jovial, invited to join them at an apartment, waitresses from the hotel, very clean girls. At another time I might have been interested.

I thought that going away, seeing some action or at least doing some important work, would make me forget. But something has changed in me, probably forever.

Can't even be sure my letters have got through. When I think she might have forgotten me…

Confusion—one moment we're staying indefinitely, then a rumour goes about that the Wehrmacht considers the region pacified and we're being transferred…

10 July

Still unclear what we are supposed to be doing here—arguments with the Wehrmacht, who do not always consider it their duty to communicate with the SS. Still nothing from her. I'm fine during the day, busy running about. At night the loneliness is awful. I'm poor company. There are kegs of beer and champagne for 1 RM, but it's useless to try to have fun.

*

11 July

Bad hangover. Only now, towards sundown, do I feel any relief. Last night, thought to drown my troubles. And today much happening, roles assigned. I am Judengeneral—in charge of Jewish matters, logistics. Not what I desired, though it entails some responsibility. The town is at least half Jewish, and has some industrial potential. Have requisitioned some vehicles. Others have been 'requisitioning' for personal profit. I dislike it, but I'll save my energy for the commanding army major here— enemy of the state. Phoned me today to say that the Jews are under the protection of the German Wehrmacht. I'll be asking Berlin to have him detained.

14 July

Couldn't write recently—my new responsibilities. Vehicle left for Radom with Dolte, Binder, Gürth and Mireck. Would have given anything to have gone myself, but at least was able to send letters and be sure of getting one back from her. Sound of their motor had hardly faded from hearing when the second in command leaps into action to make the best of Dolte's absence. Always this way—the one who doesn't usually get to give orders has been fantasising about being in charge, and suddenly we're running around, arresting people, rounding them up. Jews mostly but also some Ukrainians denounced for collaborating with the Russians. So many denunciations, gets complicated if you drag it out, you have to go with your instincts and look equally ready to shoot the snitch— that brings the truth out fast. We had them all down in a cellar, a location I'd got hold of and had cleared out that morning. Worked on them into the evening. Took a few hours off with comrade Urban to visit a woman cook— stew and new potatoes and buttermilk. Modest place but clean. Ukrainian serving-girl seemed keen to befriend me. We might have surmounted the language barrier, but my days of fooling around are over. Then back to the cellar. About fifty people down there. Most of the Jews there have been to Vienna, think it's wonderful, dream of it. Worked until 0300 hours. Hardly any sleep—woken for the execution. I desire combat, end up shooting unarmed people. 23, including two women. 0600 hours, drive out of town and down a track into the woods. Choose a suitable place. Most of them very brave. Maybe they can't believe it. Not enough shovels to go round so most of them are idle. I'm marksman in case anyone makes a run for it. Admire their composure but the scene stirs no pity in me, nothing. Just reminds me of when I faced down death— July 25 1934, in the Chancellery, looking into machine gun barrels. I'd made my choice, it was Dollfuss or us, couldn't turn back, that's not my character. My consolation was that my death would not be in vain. I was only twenty-four. In jail afterwards, lots of time to recall what I'd gone through in that decisive moment. The humiliations of those years, the guards. Now things are different, I've made it through and the world is being recast, those who would have shot me if they'd had the chance have shovels in their hands and the holes in the ground are growing bigger. Two start blubbering and I get them digging to take their minds off their troubles. Money, valuables, watches, all in one pile. Were I going to weaken, I could have done it in '34. We shoot the two women first. Six of us to shoot them. One bullet for the heart, two for the head. Two is too much for the head, blows it apart. The next pair has to lay them correctly in the grave. Goes on like this until the last pair, who sit on the edge of the grave so they can fall in. We rearrange the corpses with a pick-axe then do grave-digger duty with the shovels.

It was mid-morning, I was exhausted but the usual administrative work followed. Afternoon, earlier than expected, the car returned from Radom. Ran to it, like a child, to get my letters. Could not read them—Hauptsturmführer had me organising the new Service Building. It was 2300 hours before I was alone and could tear them open.

All this time waiting for a word from her, expecting relief, and it only brings more torment. Says she loves me, wants to be with me, feels as I do about this separation, agrees Radom has changed us both forever. Then words I can't interpret—about her insecurity, the foolishness of making promises, her uncertain future. When she writes of promises I don't know if she means his promises to her or the idea of her committing to me or my recent declarations… And then I think, well, she betrayed him, what are her vows to me worth should he turn up again? It's all up in the air and could be decided by the most trivial happening, a few words, or the presence or absence of one of us. All I can do is keep writing to her, keep myself alive through words. If I could see her, for even a minute!

Other letters—from Vienna. Read them coldly. That life is so far away and bloodless. Haven't been able to bring myself to reply. I think it would require a degree of falseness of which I'm not capable.

That was two days ago, Saturday. Between the letters and the work I haven't got much sleep.

20 July

Sunday now—no time for writing lately. As Judengeneral, am responsible for about 18,000 people. I supply the labour for various construction projects and ensure discipline. On top of this I'm supposed to train a 150-strong Ukrainian militia. The Hauptsturmführer has forbidden social visits with the Ukrainians. Pity—there are some decent households with friendly families and good country food. He doesn't object to us receiving nocturnal visits from Ukrainian girls, but that's no good to me. Actually, I don't think so much of the level of discipline among my comrades. Again, during the week a car went to Radom and everybody suddenly had an urgent reason to go. I've been wearing myself out, making sure everyone has adequate quarters, enough workers, a place to work, and still I don't have a comfortable apartment for myself. The only thing I wanted was to visit Radom, and instead I see these other men going. I was furious at being passed over. You're too important right now, said the Hauptsturmführer, and instead he sends someone who'd forgotten a toothbrush or a pair of underwear back in Radom. The Oberführer paid an unexpected visit and was delighted with progress. Of course, others got the credit for my work. Shortly after he left I decided it was time to take care of myself. There's a little Jew in the office who sorts through books and documents for us, a schoolteacher, speaks German like a Viennese, and I said to him, listen, I need an apartment, a good one, big enough for a family, and one that hasn't been looted. This is the kind of fellow who starts to shake if you look at him. He knew I meant business. Didn't take him long to locate what I needed. The apartment belonged to one of the Jewish commissars that cleared out. All I had to do was break the lock. Food still in the pantry and sheets on the beds. It's on a little street, the upper level of a two-storey house, and the front of the building faces south over a vast stretch of rolling, wooded country. The light is good and with the windows open it also receives a pleasant breeze in the middle of the day. There's a little balcony you can sit out on that I like very much. Trude would like it—a real house, not like the cramped, improvised rooms we shared in Radom.

I have to get her here, now that my prospects are good and the situation looks stable.

I sit here writing with my house fallen silent and the countryside beyond gone dark and though I allow myself hope I cannot ignore the rage I feel. Because next time too I will be far too important to be allowed go to Radom. I will send her another long, desperate letter. Something has to happen soon. I cannot stand this constant tension. I need a calm heart and a home that is filled with love. Not this endless torment.

21 July

Got home this evening before sundown, in time to sit on my little balcony and drink a couple of brandies and look over all this beautiful land, changing before my eyes as the shadows deepened, over the woodlands, over the hills, each mistier and more washed than the other, like a watercolour, the gradations registering distance until a blurred horizon. We have hemmed the Jews in and there is a curfew. Any number of them, not only the hardened

Bolsheviks, would happily cut our throats, but we have dealt decisively with the ringleaders and they act meek as sheep. I am tempted to believe that the countryside is as peaceful as it looks and that the work we do here will not be wasted. This was frontier land when I was born, in Franz Joseph's realm. The word Galicia even sounds like a faraway place but it is one that will become German too, one day, when colonists come. The woods are mostly unexploited, and agriculture remained primitive under the Poles. We still have the Austrian railroad and this region could be profitable for the German people. I will do my part. Across the road, as the hill slopes down, is some rather neglected open land. I have decided to have some greenhouses built and I already have them digging the foundations (I will have some walls, concrete or brick, about eighty centimetres high), and will have an orchard planted too. I don't know how long this posting will last—I might be in the Caucasus next year, or on the other side of the Urals—but at least I will have fresh produce further into the autumn, and the work will be appreciated by the next administrator. I am encouraging my comrades to take similar initiatives and putting the workforce at their disposal. The more food we produce here, the more can be sent east, towards those fighting for our future.

As I make this place comfortable, as I watch my Jews tending the garden and making it beautiful, I think of the smile on Trude's face when I show it to her for the first time. It is all a gift to her. Its only worth is as an offering to lay before her. Oh, I know that sounds terribly grand. But I feel it, and in this world that has been thrown into such thrilling, terrible disorder it is she who guides me. Like it says in the Bible—without love we are nothing. How my mother would be proud of me. I haven't touched a Bible for years. But I remember a few things.

Answered today the letters from my wife and remitted to her 180 RM.

22 July

Yesterday, waiting for the vehicle to return from Radom, constantly glancing out the window, asking for news, and it was delayed and only arrived today. More exasperating lines from Trude. In one sentence I feel her love, hear her voice as I heard it when we lay together. In the next I sense she has betrayed me already. She can betray her fiancé so readily so why not me? Then I try to calm down, tell myself I'm being too emotional when really I should be thinking of what is to be done. Because it is entirely possible that she loves me and is only waiting for me to bring her here. A violent outburst, telling her it is over, is exactly what will push her into the arms of another.

Can't take any more of this. Games being played. She sent on some things from Radom, including pictures of my wife and children. All right, I get it, pictures of the children, of course I want those. The picture of my wife? I can only take it as a reproach.

Stores broken into, tyres of official vehicles slashed. Haggling with the Jewish Council over the workforce. Jews running away when I go investigate. Will carry my pistol at all times from now on, for such occasions. Announced I need a hundred Jews to report within an hour or I'd shoot the same number. Got my workers, and a surplus, and had twenty shot for those who'd run away. Incident later with a Ukrainian guard who berated our Jews, who were at this point cooperating and locating stores of lost material. Sensed pilfering by the Ukrainians. Worked on this guard personally. He fell down a few times before I got the truth out of him.

At the end of my tether. Will be raising the question of Trude being transferred here. If it fails, I'll ask to be replaced. I'll write to her and tell her how things stand so she is in no doubt. She cannot say I am not clear. I am offering her my throat, to kiss or to cut. So be it. Goodnight my love. I look at your picture and I extinguish the light.

24 July

My time with Trude feels like the only real thing that has ever happened to me. Everything about it has a heightened intensity. The words she spoke and even their intonation come back to me, like the memory of piano notes. I remember that unnaturally bright morning with the sun breaking through the window, lighting our naked bodies, heating up that little room. I kissed her beautiful ribcage, her hard belly, then drew back to look at her—I could see every detail, every tiny golden hair stood out individually, illuminated in that trembling light. Yes—the light was literally trembling. The sunlight was heating the floorboards and the sun shone through the warm rising air and trembled on the white wall.

Dear Trude, everything that we do in life, with our hearts, is the making of something. That is how we make it real. This is all our lives can possibly amount to, these acts of love.

You don't know what love is until you fall to your knees before a woman, and discard your old life. You realise your old life was worth nothing, and you throw it away and embrace the new life.

28 July

Not enough sleep. The little I write goes into my letters to Trude. The weekend slipped by and I hardly noticed. Got some good carpets brought in. Comrade Urban and I had a meeting on Friday with some Slovak lieutenants, men of real character, very religious. No comparison with the Ukrainians, who cannot be trusted. The Slovaks spoke good German and it was easy to get along. Informed us they'd found an unguarded arms depot and we went to investigate and I detonated the lock—hundreds of rifles, ammo and grenades and machine guns, all belonging to the Wehrmacht, and just as we were going through the inventory a Wehrmacht vehicle drives up—great embarrassment on their part, excuses. Also last week, an insane episode—summoned by Ukrainian villagers to a site outside town where the Reds massacred some Ukrainians. We arrive, there's a Ukrainian priest, they're reburying the victims, giving them some dignity, then the priest tells us the worst thing is that fake Jewish papers had been planted on the dead. The place begins to seem familiar. Then it hits me—these were our legitimately shot Jews, about twenty-five of them. The papers stank. Had them soaked in petrol and incinerated.

Still no chance of going to Radom. Due a visit here from Governor-General Frank and have to make sure everything is in order. The logistical side of things is a challenge. These Jews have to be fed if they're to work. When the fighting's over we'll solve the problem properly—send them east. They'll learn how to get their own food from the fields and the forests. For now it must all be done for them by the Judengeneral and between this and training the Ukrainian militia I am making myself hard to replace. Letting it be understood that I need time in Radom or I will officially request to be relieved. My longer-term hope is to get Trude here. Confident that my standing here will appeal to her. I am no longer just anybody, after all. Her last letter, so loving and open, full of youthful seriousness, yet wise and practical—she even analyses my situation, my marriage, shows she understands me. I just felt love, passionate love, and so much hope as I read. And still I have nightmare moments when the room darkens and the air is sucked out of it at the thought that she is hiding something from me and I feel the floor about to give way beneath me. If she were to deceive me I would lose faith in humankind and not recover it. With my last letter I sent her a love scene, a miniature from the Baroque era, quite valuable and I'm sure she'll adore it. My little Jew, the schoolmaster, found it for me. He's handy, appraises artwork, books, and we're putting together an inventory. He's a good painter. The Bolsheviks had him doing propaganda murals. When I told him I knew about that, his mouth started moving wordlessly and I think he thought I was about to shoot him. I put him to work beautifying the Gestapo club.

*

1 August

Great progress made in my affairs yesterday, following a dinner invitation to Dolte's apartment. Our comrade Driese was there too and when I arrived Dolte had a letter from his girlfriend in Radom on the table and was openly discussing his personal affairs. He is making little progress with his divorce despite having a whole team of lawyers pursuing it in Vienna. The slow back and forth of communications and the turmoil of this summer confound things. I said very little but after comrade Driese left he offered wine and cigarettes and I confessed my own troubles. Dolte knew about Trude, but not the seriousness of the matter. He reassured me that he would provide every support for Trüdchen's transfer here. It could be done on a temporary basis at first. I was surprised how easy he made it sound. And on top of that I got an assurance that I would be on the trip to Radom on Saturday the 9th. Today I was in good spirits, it was an easy day for my Ukrainian militia. I had to speak harshly to my Jew, the painter. He looked ready to faint though I make sure he gets well fed. He's been taking his rations to his friends in the ghetto. I told him it would end badly for him if he can't do his work. He got the message. I was gentle with my Jews but the uniforms for the militia were not ready so I told the council I'd shoot five tailors for sabotage if the work is not completed by midday tomorrow.

2 August

The uniforms were ready. Governor Frank not coming—I could have gone to Radom. With my comrades who are going I'm sending a letter to Trude—a more confident one this time. In it I give her instructions. That is the tone of it anyway. Whether she will play the part is another matter. She has a ring on her finger that needs discarding. To my wife, sending RM 180 and toys for the children (some things I've had my Jews carve from wood and other baubles). And constant work—buildings made fit for habitation, repairs and improvements everywhere. I feel as though I am building a city sometimes and even when I am not doing it my imagination is still aroused and envisioning the evolution of my project.

3 August

Working at the equestrian centre in the morning. Looking good now, getting my painter Jew, my general artistic handyman, to effect some final flourishes. Promised Dolte I'd show him how to ride. Then in the afternoon couldn't resist taking one of the horses out—a solitary patrol through the hinterland that could have cost me my life. First I passed some Gypsies. You would not know from the filth and disorder in which they live that this nation has centuries of experience in making encampments. We ignored each other. I continued downriver for some distance and was about to veer into the woods when I detected a number of men withdrawing into it hastily. I had my pistol but was wary of drawing it and giving the impression I was hunting them as for all I knew there was a gun trained on me from somewhere among the trees. At this point I detected activity on the other bank also, as well as horses and signs of an encampment. I went a little further down and forded the river and approached them.

These ones didn't run and I was surprised to see women and children. Perhaps a dozen people in all. I approached casually and made conversation. Poles, but not from the area. I make out many more figures lurking in the bushes and behind trees. Refugees, deserters, fugitives—impossible to tell. They're as wary as I am. I decide against going further downstream, deeper into the woods, and opt to make for a ridge and circle back towards town on higher ground. All for the sake of pretending to this rabble that I knew where I was going—and a mistake, as it was steeper and more treacherous than I anticipated and my horse kept slipping. At one point he fell and threw me and rolled and I was lucky not to get crushed. When he went to rise his left forefoot would have smashed my skull had I not punched it aside. The right hoof struck my chest. Made a report when I got back. We will now patrol the woods. The country appears pacified but keeping it that way depends on our attitude. We are being watched, and the only thing keeping this irregular population at bay is fear. I'm euphoric despite the pain from my tumble; yesterday the second in command told me we need shorthand typists and no reason why Miss Trude Segel should not be one of them. I will travel soon to Radom to attend to this matter. Right now, Dolte has some wild women in his apartment, but my own door is bolted.

I remember my first night with you, Trude, and the morning. We drank coffee, both ragged from drink and lack of sleep and the strangeness of being together. Complete disorientation. We had no idea what it meant. I wanted you so much. But couldn't say it. We had transgressed. So what could I say the morning after? The coffee was finished and it was time to go. The attack east had been launched the day before. Your fiancé was fighting there and soon I would be too. It was only a matter of time before I was transferred. I wanted to say, Now you are mine. But how could I burden you with the terrible intensity of that, even were it what you wanted to hear? I did not want to hurt you. How could I tell anymore right or wrong, true from false? But in the end I did surrender. I tried to say something true. As I was about to leave, I held your hands and leaned my forehead against yours and I said, 'When we made love last night, I felt you were mine.' I'd met you too late. Time was out of joint. It was hard to get a grip on the fact that I wore a uniform, that the tide was pulling me east, that before I met you I had lived an entire life, in other cities, to remember the sacrifices I'd made for the ideals of National Socialism, that we were now in some town in Poland… I got up to leave. I put on my coat. It was reassuring for a moment, that series of discrete acts. But then we were standing at the closed doorway, embracing, kissing and not wanting to let each other go for what would be the last time. Tears rolled down your face but your crying made no sound. I cleaned a tear from each of your cheeks with my lips. Salty. Some kind of gesture. Your blood, your tears, why not? I'm glad you're suffering, I told you. Now I don't feel so alone. We kissed a little more. Well, I said, this could go on all day. I could have dragged it out, seen how many tears I was worth. Come on, we're adults, I said. Whatever that meant. That we were above pointless emotion, I suppose, and that shortly we'd be pulling ourselves together, and sweeping up and discarding the mess we'd made.

I went down to the street. I didn't know if I was to go right or left. I think I went right. It was very bright. I was in a foreign country. The streets were strange to me, the people, the vehicles and horses. I had to stop by my quarters, to wash and shave before I reported for duty. I no longer knew who I was. And it was not true that you were my love. You loved somebody else. You had already told me that. It seemed incongruous, something I could momentarily forget, but it was a fact.

And now I lie here, propped up with pillows. My ribs are badly bruised and it hurts when I breathe. I think of all I have been through over the past weeks and how the world has changed and I look at your picture and can hardly believe that soon you will be here with me and that now nothing and nobody can keep us apart.

4 August

Other moments. Woke in the night, jolt of paranoia. What game is she playing? How can this end well? A woman who can have any man. She has all the power. I have none. This in an element in my intoxication. I fear for myself.

Slept badly because of the bruising. But the pace of work does not slacken.

5 August

The deal is done—official permission for wives and 'brides' to come. I think also of Vienna. My comrades know my position. At another time it would have been awkward but formalities count for so much less in this new situation, where our responsibilities are so much greater. The very thought of Vienna. I will have to regularise my situation shortly. My lodgings are looking well. Hosted Dolte and some other comrades yesterday evening. The house-Jewess put together a good feed—fried chicken, new potatoes, cucumber salad, then raspberries for dessert. I had some wine. Urban, my happily married comrade, commented that the only thing missing was our loved ones. A happy family life has been denied me, for now. To bring my wife here? To play that role and bury everything vital? No, there are moments when you must choose between your real life and the comfortable, compromised one that you never inhabit, not truly. I will take the road of trouble. On Saturday I go to Radom. The only one who can derail my plans now is Trude. But I must continue, until the end.

Think I'll get my Jew to do some painting in here. Some finer work to cheer up the walls.

7 August

Sweet music on the radio. If I close my eyes I could be back home. I imagine my dear friends and comrades, scattered now, hearing these same sounds in different places, pausing and thinking of one another. And I think about Trude of course, in her room in Radom, listening and perhaps thinking of me. In two days I will be on the road again, heading towards her, and I imagine arriving and looking for her, and finding her, and her being as eager as I am to go somewhere quickly where we can be alone to kiss and caress each other wordlessly. Perhaps she will be at work and I will have to wait. I imagine also that she is out, being entertained by one of my comrades. Yes, that occurs to me also. I'll ask Schwarz to vacate my old apartment for me for the evening. Otherwise it will be Trude's little place.

Oh, she is a woman, but in other ways she is a girl, I fear, and has no strength, and all I have had these weeks to send her are my words of love and strength. My life depends on what happens in the next seventy-two hours.

Work constantly, to quell my nerves. Convicted, very quickly, nine Ukrainians of looting. Probably not the worst offenders. But they will be an example.

13 August

The Radom trip—thought it would never happen. Even up to the last moment, when Sturmbannführer Heine turned up with our Hauptführer, I feared it would mean some nonsensical task had been invented to keep me from my destiny, like a dream where you are always frustrated, where your anxious mind is focused upon a jewel but the road towards it is by the second getting longer and more scattered with obstacles. What I've learned these weeks is that when you think you can endure no more they'll invent another twist, another variety of torture. We left after sundown and I stared ahead at that funnel of headlights all through the night and the sun came up over the countryside like something remembered from a previous life, then we were approaching Radom. I leapt from the car and in a single second, as Trüdchen clung to me with all her strength, I knew I was saved, that all my doubts were the phantoms that visit you in sleep, and since then I have been brimming with peace, overflowing with it. She rapidly agreed to come here. Her only concern was her parents, but they will have to accept that the rules in this world have changed. We slept at her place and already at

1700 hours the next day I had to leave, reaching Drohobycz at six in the morning, exhausted but able to inform Dolte that we could now effect Trude's transfer.

15 August

Took Dolte and other comrades on a mounted patrol. Our spirits are good and soon the women will be here. Dolte has the making of a good horseman. The Gypsies still linger but the other transients have moved elsewhere, or gone deeper into the woods. The rest is work. Parties of Jews working through the night to get the offices and lodging properly ready for the arrival of the women. Trüdchen will live with me, but certain formalities must be observed— she and the other yet-unmarried women will be allocated their own quarters.

Some executions. Senkovsky is a sadist. His interrogations turn lethal. His prerogative. Still, you wouldn't want him at your table.

17 September

Tomorrow she will come. It is finally happening. After so many delays, after the nervous exhaustion of the past months, I have moments of utter desolation. As though I have been playing a crazy game, have suppressed all the usual fears with a drug and they are waiting to come back. The yawning emptiness that follows drunken excitement, when you know you will pay with shame for your profligacy. You think, surely falling in love must be followed by a reckoning, and the longer it is put off the more shameful it will be. This worm of doubt, burrowing into you, telling you that the new world you glimpsed was never real.

These moments of weakness. The test of our character is what we build, and continue to build, even in difficult moments, when we are tired and dispirited, when others get credit, or when our comrades are insufficiently grateful. I feel I am creating something of value here and it is an enduring satisfaction to watch the progress. More accommodation for our comrades and staff. My Ukrainians, fewer in number, more reliable. The equestrian centre now running beautifully, with over seventy horses and regular patrols into the countryside. Riding hall, stables, garages, apartments for comrades, administrative buildings—I see to it all. Things are moving with the divorce. I leave it to the lawyers. I will have the children brought here. They will miss their mother at first, of course, but this is how it has to be. I can't have them raised by her family, apart from the fact that they would be poisoned against me. It would not be so bad for Matilde but for Dieter it would be a disaster. A boy needs his father. His love, of course, but also discipline.

We need more Germans here, eventually. I keep my Jews busy and fed, but the ghetto will have to be cleaned out. I don't know if there is a disinfectant strong enough. Perhaps fire. The situation is unsustainable. The sooner we can send them east the better. We will have to maintain them through the winter now, but I can't see them being retained past spring. Leningrad is now encircled, so is Kiev. Moscow will be next. Soon the Red Army will crumble. They surrender in the hundreds of thousands. More mouths to feed.

A chill in the air now. As the sun settles in the evening the fading light brings out other colours in the woods, warmer pinks and ambers as the leaves of some of the trees begin to turn, and this will intensify in the coming weeks, and I imagine sitting here with Trude, watching it. I have the doors to the balcony open now, and have moved my little writing desk so that I can look out over it. The breeze that enters is cool, and I have a glass of white wine, and the radio is playing.

Think I'll get my Jew to do something on the walls of the little room. I envisage a nursery or playroom for the children. Some scenes from fairy tales, or animals. Dieter likes cats. Yes, that would be nice.

This is a semi-fictionalised rewriting of the diary of Felix Landau (1910-1983). He was joined in Drohobycz by Gertrude Segel (Trude) shortly after this account breaks off. Landau divorced his first wife and married Trude in 1943. They had one child together and were divorced in 1946.

The above account has respected the essential facts regarding Landau's activities as Judengeneral and the chronology of historical events. Landau supervised the exploitation of the Drohobycz ghetto for labour until most of its inhabitants were deported to Belzec extermination camp in 1942. One of Landau's personal slaves was the short story writer and visual artist Bruno Schulz, until Schulz's death by shooting in November 1942.

Landau was arrested in Stuttgart in 1962 and charged with war crimes. His diary was used in evidence at his trial. He was sentenced to life imprisonment but pardoned in 1973.

Bells in Bright Air

Down in the street a dog was barking and I lay in the dark for hours listening to it. I staged a dawn raid on the medicine chest and went back to bed. Apaches descended on me in in black and white, screaming, and I shot them off their horses.

When I woke the dog was still barking. The sound echoed in the concrete canyon of the street. I showered and drank a coffee and sat down at my desk and sharpened my pencils. When I could no longer bear the noise, I took my rifle from where it rests along the top of the bookcase, stepped out onto my balcony, took aim and fired. No more barking. An old man leaning on his balcony on the other side of the street had seen it happen. He gave me the thumbs up. I nodded to him in acknowledgement and went back inside. I returned the rifle to its place on top of the bookshelf.

I sat down at my desk. It was finally quiet but I found I was not ready for work after all. My desk faces the window and I get little done, now that the weather is warmer and the door is open to the little balcony. I was thinking about dogs. About the funny way they will gaze into your soul, like a lover or a newborn. The thoughts were starting to connect and I was about to get something done when I was disturbed again by noise, this time a rumble of what sounded like obscenities and threats being uttered by someone in the street. From his brutal diction, I knew what the man would look like. They come cutting through this way, slouching like Neanderthals, sometimes a worn-out woman trailing several paces behind. No jobs, these brutes, but they like to breed. You hear them on the radio going on about the low paid and the disadvantaged, but I can tell you, they are not all very nice people. Read about it in Solzhenitsyn, how in the camps the authorities let the criminal scum slit the throats of the bourgeois prisoners with impunity. The people with manners, you see, had lost the war. They had refined themselves into a state of helplessness.

I stood up, took the gun back down from the bookcase, checked my ammo and took up position on the balcony. I took aim for just a little longer than I did with the dog, at the base of the man's skull, and he fell face-forward onto the footpath. There was indeed a woman in tow, and she stopped and leaned over to inspect him—obviously he wasn't getting up again—and then she turned and looked up and saw me. The gun was slung over my shoulder at this point, and I posed no immediate threat to anybody. She gave me a timid little wave and smiled. She was short a few teeth. I raised my hand in acknowledgement. A guy had just parked on the footpath opposite and he was looking up at me too. He stood beside his vehicle, keys dangling from one finger, unsure what would happen next. Hey, I boomed at him, Don't park on the footpath, old people and kids need to use it!

In fact, other vehicles were already parked along the footpath and his van made no difference. But after I went back inside I heard his engine starting up and the van driving away. I put my gun back on top of the bookshelf.

So much for the dead guy, I thought, sitting down at my desk. So much for his muscles and so much for his big mouth. Maybe his mother would cry for him. Nobody born can't make their mama cry. I still wanted to get some work done, but there was no longer any point. I'd just be warming up when it would be time to stop. I cut my fingernails instead. Ideally I should have steeped them in warm water first, and pushed the cuticles back. And why shouldn't we take care of our hands, these sensitive instruments that have evolved for millions of years, to the point where we can do neurosurgery or play the Moonlight Sonata with our eyes gently closed. But I didn't bother with the cuticles. I just clipped the nails. I gathered all the little bits off the floor and disposed of them. Then I finished cleaning up around the house, the usual stuff, and waited for her to come back.

She arrived home some hours later in her heels and office gear. I told her she was looking great. She asked what I'd been doing all day. Nothing much, I said, and she made a face, even though the house was gleaming and there was a pot of food in the fridge that just needed reheating. She's gone a lot with work, sometimes days at a time, and I don't even ask any more. We don't always talk. Or we talk, and it's not always what we're saying. Or else we say things and it looks like the world is about to explode, then we pretend nothing was said and she puts on her make-up and heads out again. But that's marriage, I suppose. Or maybe it isn't. I don't know. Then she was in the shower, I could hear the water going, I was gazing out the window and I could see by the shadows it was time to get the little girl. I didn't have to look at the clock. I always know by the light. So I was out the door, and the woman was still having her big long shower. She thinks it's funny, me scrubbing the floor while she's running around, but she's going to get a surprise one of these days.

I went down and they'd cleared the corpse from the street, no sign it had even happened.

It was a short walk, fifteen minutes, to the playschool. Usually I get there a bit early and I walk around. Or else I wait outside, and I visualise her waking from her nap. They give the children little cakes after they get up then send them out to play.

This time, from over the high wall, I could hear them in the playground, their voices like bells in the bright air, and I stood outside for a long time, listening for the sound of her voice among the others. Finally, I pressed the buzzer and they opened the automatic gate and I went in and she ran to me like she always does, her face pure sunshine, and I hunkered down, so we could embrace. She's three. She's one of the smallest kids there. I worry about her being among bigger rougher kids, even though I know it's stupid to worry. And then I said goodbye to the childcare professionals and we headed home, holding hands. After a few minutes she always wants me to carry her and I hoist her up and she likes the view and it's easier to talk then over the noise of the traffic, our faces close, sometimes touching, especially the occasional days I'm shaved clean, because she doesn't like what she calls my spikes. We get along great. No two people get along better. If her mother thinks she's going to interfere with that she's got a nasty shock coming. In this realm, there is dizzy confusion between the man and the woman. You love a woman the way a bee loves a flower. It lasts as long as it needs to last. The flame is hot and brief and afterwards the cold negotiations begin. But the way you love your kid only grows and grows. Do you know why humans are right-handed? Because you hold your child next to your heart, where it can feel that reassuring pulse, from the moment it is born. Look at anyone carrying their child, even when it's bigger — they carry it on their left. So the right is free, and that has evolved to be the business hand.

The tricky bit of this journey is the dictator's boulevard. When I was a boy they bulldozed much of the old town and put a big road through the ruins. The pedestrian lights change from green to red before you have time to cross and amid the growling traffic we become that herd of nervous wildebeest on the Discovery Channel who've sniffed a lion in the grass, stampeding each other's heels. One taxi driver was leaning on the horn, trying to scatter us so he could jam his foot down again. He had one elbow propped lazily on an open window, cigarette dangling between his fingers. It was this boorish pose that did it. Obviously I don't take my rifle out with me when I go for a walk but I do carry a discreet little thing holstered at my hip, beneath my coat. Call it a lady's gun, I don't care. I wasn't interested in bullets through the windscreen or any B-movie dramatics. I just popped one in him through the open side-window, and I had holstered and rejoined the crowd hurrying to the safety of the far footpath even before his head had slumped forward, onto the steering wheel. Somebody patted my back, somebody else mumbled a few words of approval and the general feeling was that I had done something that needed to be done a long time ago. Then the moment was lost in the motion and noise of the city, and as I walked away all that remained was the car stopped at the lights and the other drivers backed up and blaring their horns at him. It had been quick but my little one guessed something was up and said, Daddy, what's the matter with that man?

He's not dead, I told her. He's just asleep.

I don't want her to know about these things. I don't want her to see any fights. I wish both of us could stay kids forever. Sometimes I wonder how it all happened so fast.

A giant silver coin of a full moon was hanging low in the cool blue sky at the end of the dictator's boulevard, gleaming with impossible clean light above the tortured city, and I said to her, astonished, Look at that!—and walked into the woman in front of me.

Look where you're going! she snarled, over her shoulder.

I apologised immediately. It had been my fault.

My Life in the City

A small backpack was open on the bed. I was filling it with items of clothing. Morning sun hit the bedspread and the varnished floorboards. A 1930s art-deco block, fourth floor. Out the window, a view over a promiscuous jumble of buildings, various ages and styles, afloat in early summer green.

When I lived there first, three years before, the room was empty. A mattress on the ground. I would read in the evenings, pillows against the wall, in a pool of lamplight, as the birds in the trees went quiet and the sky turned dark.

Then I met Carmen. The mattress became a double bed. A dressing table with a mirror appeared and then a chest of drawers, and a massive wardrobe.

Now I was getting out.

I rented, cheap, from an old friend who lived abroad. His father, the previous occupant, had died. Before moving in, those three years earlier, I had helped the relatives bin and burn and scrub. We hauled out papers and books and furniture and fixed leaking taps and replaced cracked windows. And as we did this work, I thought of the books the man had read, left stacked and yellowing on their shelves, worthless even for second-hand bookshops, and of the sheaves of letters he had received and kept, the correspondents now dead, and the boxes of black-and-white photographs of people dressed like 1950s movie stars. The pictures on the wall, the worn and mismatched accumulation of furniture, all the useless knick-knacks and souvenirs—you couldn't tell what they once signified or if an antique shop would hang a tag on them. I'd read that in India a man of good family prepared for death by shedding his burden of household possessions and obligations, and withdrawing to a quiet place to reflect. It seemed a better way to go.

And so I moved in, carrying my single bag of belongings. On my first night alone there I crept about like a nervous guest, afraid to make a sound. The apartment still held the imprint of the dead man. The parquet around the doorways was eroded by a lifetime of his footsteps. The walls were yellowed by nicotine and the ancient dust of the city. I lay down on my mattress on the ground and had trouble falling asleep.

But I slept deeply and when I woke the room was flooded with morning sunlight and I felt immortal. I was making my way, claiming my own space. In that city of brutalist apartment blocks and screaming boulevards I had got myself a touch of class in a quiet neighbourhood close to the centre. I thought I might stay there forever, or until I got something even better.

I sanded the boards by hand and varnished them and painted the walls. I turned up the music and had friends over. I brought women back. Had long evenings alone reading, and stood on the balcony and watched the rooftops and the yards and distant blocks under different skies, different lights, imagining myself the one stable element in the ever-shifting world, there to give it wholeness by observing and remembering it.

I met Carmen at a reception. I was telling somebody about a play I'd seen and then she was standing next to me in a black dress, a long string of pearls looped to fall between her breasts, and she was saying theatre was fine, but what about illiteracy levels among marginalised groups? I had no interest in marginalised groups. My life in the city was moving along nicely. I had written a prize-winning play and then a movie screenplay. I was covering my meagre expenses until my next big break by co-writing a TV soap with three other people. She told me about her NGO. I told her I wished to learn more about the poor. She offered her card.

She moved in three weeks later. By then the pearls had been returned to their owner, and I learned she was broke. She was a volunteer with the organisation I'd assumed she directed. I was proud to support her good work.

My first lesson about the poor was that Carmen did not wish to live like them. She insisted I buy a washing machine. That was when I began to notice the apartment closing in, as I stepped from the shower, squeezing between the newly installed machine and the toilet bowl. I had been content to do my laundry manually, steeping it in a bucket in the bath and stirring it with my foot when I showered.

Then wardrobes were required for Carmen's clothes. So many clothes she could not get around to wearing them all. Not enough days in the year. It seemed as though every time she left the house she came back with more frippery. And she wanted to know what I thought. I always thought it was fine. Everything looked good on her. But these items needed to be stashed somewhere. Same with the shoes. Soon I was tripping over them. They even turned up on bookshelves.

I bought a drill and a handsaw and put up shelves from floor to ceiling in the alcove in the bedroom. I was proud of my handiwork and it solved the shoe problem for a while. Then there were more shoes.

And when we took a trip together we needed keepsakes, souvenirs, trinkets. Kitchen implements and appliances were a practical requirement. And then there were presents for birthdays, name-days, Christmases, or as spontaneous gestures, and since we already had everything, we had to get it twice. We had a teapot, so we got another one, so ornamental and delicate it was useless for brewing tea and just sat on a shelf. Decorative jars and bowls multiplied throughout the apartment, on windowsills and shelves and ledges, and they filled up with shells, hairclips, cosmetics, nailfiles, bangles, perfume bottles, earrings, ticket stubs, ribbons, pens, pencils, coins, matchboxes, feathers, face creams, essential oils, buttons, pins and coloured stones. The apartment was a vortex, a black hole, sucking in shoes and fabric and baubles from throughout the universe.

The neighbours were mostly elderly. The basement, where they pickled cabbage in vats in the winter, was not vast enough for their junk. It spilled onto the common landings and the stairwell. One day, a widow on the second floor clutched my elbow and drew me into her apartment to climb on a chair to retrieve a box from atop a wardrobe. Her balcony was clogged with cupboards, boxes and old fridges, blocking out the light.

That night I woke abruptly. Carmen woke too and asked what was wrong.

'I can't breathe,' I said.

'Open the window.'

'It *is* open.'

Her organisation helped victims of domestic violence. I got involved too. I'd arrive home after an afternoon concocting love-complications for TV and papers would be laid out on the kitchen table for me or a document open on the laptop. I became skilled at making pitches to the PR departments of banks and luxury hotels for a few drops of their 'corporate citizenship' budget.

The money from the screenplay was gone and I wasn't writing any more prize-winning plays. When not occupied with TV drama and philanthropy, I was cooking and cleaning and shopping and doing the laundry and paying bills. Carmen reacted acidly when I suggested she might take a turn washing the floor. She was not a servant and if I was neurotic about dust—'anal' was the word used—then I could hire a cleaning lady.

Sometimes, when cleaning the toilet perhaps, or scrubbing a stovetop, I would become quietly angry. But I had to acknowledge that she was not lazy. She was fighting the evil in the world. She was busy putting everyone else's house in order.

*

My pal Ritzi had a bar. The owner was living on a beach in Thailand and Ritzi was in charge until he decided to come back. It was an odd watering hole. You'd take a stool and to one side of you were maybe a couple of girls concerned about the welfare of street dogs and on the other a biker with a greying ponytail who'd urge you to read *Mein Kampf* with an open mind. One afternoon we had the place to ourselves and Ritzi was behind the bar, polishing some glasses that looked already bright. We were both drinking red wine from tumblers and I was talking:

'See Ritz, a little boy on a beach, he'll pick up a rock and throw it in the water. The rock is an extension of his power. But the little girl will collect the pretty shells and stones, put them in her pocket and bring them home. Women want to possess beauty, make it their personal attribute. And men want to possess women. Beauty is just the language that expresses her fertility.'

Ritzi nodded. He played bass in a band that hadn't gone anywhere but he still gigged. He had been single for some time, as far as I knew.

'The biological imperative, you mean. So he can spread his seed.'

'The woman, reasonably enough, wants certain assurances before she'll consent to be knocked up. So the male, in competition with all other males, gets caught up in the world of activity to demonstrate he's a practical and capable fellow. Next thing, he's building cities, accumulating goods and there's holy matrimony, and he's going around being civilised. How much of this did the poor bastard understand? He wanted to feel alive, and now he's in jail. He can recall begging on his knees to be let in the gates.

And this constraint on the male, the deal he makes with the female to be permitted to stand at the altar of her beauty, erupts in orgies of violence. The armies of Genghis Khan, waves of horsemen, burning it all down, one city after another, breaking and entering, taking what they want without saying please or thank you or wiping their boots.'

I took a big drink at the end of this speech. You'd think I'd just ridden the long hot dusty road from Mongolia myself.

I placed my empty glass on the counter. Ritzi lifted an eyebrow. I nodded. He refilled. The bubbles swirled in the dark liquid and settled. We had not exhausted the subject. It was still afternoon.

The night before we split, Carmen accused me of being attracted to the wife of a friend of mine. We'd been out visiting this couple. They lived on an upper floor of a standard brutalist block with a view of other such blocks, and as evening fell the lighted windows looked like rows of TV screens tuned to the same show. Our hosts had queued with other young couples in the open-plan area of a bank to outline their credit requirements, and had as a result succeeded in jamming a lot of stuff under their low ceiling. It was mostly from Ikea, which had landed on the edge of town some years before like a giant spacecraft from another civilisation.

Carmen made the accusation, or bitter observation, in the street, as we were going home. I waved down a cab and we got in. We said nothing for the duration of the ride. The charge detonated at home as we were removing our shoes in the hall. The fight wore on through hours of darkness side by side in bed.

Once these sessions started, I could find no way to end them. Every word I spoke would turn out to be incriminatory, provocative and combustible. Afterwards, I could never remember exactly what was said. These fights drew on another register of utterance, slick and darting, and when she'd demand I explain what I'd meant two comments back or two days before, I never had a clue—a Hydra nightmare where you faced the monster bravely and decapitated it while mutant versions multiplied in the shadows.

Months earlier, burned out, argued out, I told her if she didn't shut up I'd strangle her and, in a moment of high dramatic vindication that made me detest her, she sat bolt upright and turned on the bedside light. I had said the unsayable, I had threatened her with physical violence, which was proof of my underlying aggression. The light was above my head and the lecture continued, but you would have needed a degree in clinical psychology to follow it. She'd veer off onto these jargonised loony tangents, delivering horseshit fabrications as though they were the incontrovertible truths of the social sciences. It made no sense to ask if she believed her own rhetoric—the possibility, let's say, that my smouldering patriarchal rage could drive me to asphyxiate her. It was thrilling enough for her to articulate such things, to aggressively turn up the heat even as she posited her feminine vulnerability. She had proven on a number of occasions that my behaviour was 'abusive' and by the end of each inquisition I was so worn out the verdict seemed to stand.

Still, I regretted telling Carmen I would throttle her, and swore to her I'd never say it again. And I never did.

But I sometimes thought it, on those occasions late at night when I was so tired I could no longer formulate a coherent sentence, and she was in full righteous flow, and I would beg her to stop talking.

Please, Carmen, I would say. Please stop.

Another night, several months before we split, I was leaning against the bar in Ritzi's. Carmen was there too, a touch of class against the background grunge, and Ritzi was posing me a riddle:

'What's the hole in a man's ass called? An anus, right?'

'Right'.

'So what's the hole in a woman's ass called?'

'What?'

'A bonus.'

We laughed, then laughed at each other laughing, and when it seemed to be over Ritzi looked at me and said *bonus* and it started again.

But Carmen wasn't laughing. With a stiff smile she asked Ritzi if the joke meant the male was the anatomical standard and the female a deviation? Or that a woman was just a series of holes for the male to plug?

'Come on, Carmen,' I said. 'It's a joke... '

'Like Freud said, where there's a joke, there's a problem. It's a joke about women.'

Ritzi shrugged.

'I do have a problem with women,' said Ritzi. 'I don't have much luck with them and I suppose it's my own fault.'

Carmen was for a moment disarmed by Ritzi's lack of swagger. Then he asked her: 'How many feminists does it take to change a lightbulb?'

'I don't know.'

'One. And it isn't funny.'

Carmen smiled, but she did not laugh.

After that, I only saw Ritzi without Carmen. So almost never. I was busy with my job at the TV station and helping Carmen with her philanthropy. And I had my housework too.

We argued through the night, the final one we spent together, until we lay on our backs, exhausted, looking at the ceiling. At about four o'clock in the morning Carmen said to me, her voice now steady:

'What would happen if I got pregnant? You don't want to have children with me, do you?'

I saw how neat it had just become.

'No. I can't say I do.'

It's a long journey from the first night of passion to the first sleepless night arguing about how to raise the kids, as some wise man once put it. At least we would get to skip the bit with the kids.

The sun was coming up, illuminating the walls.

The apartment was no longer mine. It would have been unreasonable to ask her move all that stuff. Her shoes alone—overflowing from their alcove, poking out from under the bed, invading the bookshelf, lined up on top of the wardrobe—would have needed a removal crew. A brief exchange followed, concerning practicalities.

Yet still, it tore me up, standing in the bedroom that final morning, the small backpack open on the bed, looking at all her junk. Our life together, our love, had got terribly wrapped up in it.

*

I waited until after eleven so as not to wake Ritzi too early then climbed the dirty stairwell, past walls of flaking plaster and windows that were either cracked or broken. He opened the door in the shorts and baggy T-shirt he'd slept in. It was a one-room attic apartment with a kitchen nook with a counter and a stool. There was a little sofa and an oval Formica-top coffee table, a tall lamp with a lopsided dusty fabric shade and a director's chair by the porthole window. The floor was unvarnished boards, covered with a patina of grime. A narrow mattress with a knot of bedding lay against one wall and beside the mattress was an acoustic guitar and an electric bass connected to a speaker. The surfaces— the table, the kitchen counter, the top of the speaker and much of the floor—were invisible beneath papers, books, magazines, plastic bags, jars, empty food containers, plates and bowls and cups and other items. He had been breakfasting on crackers with peanut butter and strawberry jam. A joint was rolled and waiting in the ashtray. I rinsed out a cup and helped myself to coffee and hacked at sugar caked at the bottom of the bowl. I transferred some books and magazines from the sofa to the oval table.

I sat down on the lumpy sofa, told Ritzi I was homeless.

He lit up and puffed smoke.

'What happened?'

'It went sour.'

'Overnight?'

'Gradually. Then suddenly.'

'But that was your apartment.'

'I couldn't kick her out. She has no money. I threw in my job too.'

'Huh?'

'So I don't end up paying her rent. Or going back because I miss my apartment.'

'Smart.'

'And she said I had a thing for Dia.'

Dia was my friend's wife. The couple Carmen and I had visited the night before.

'That's crazy,' said Ritzi.

'No it isn't. It's true.'

Ritzi said nothing for a moment. He was embarrassed.

'Want some?'

'No.'

He took a few drags then stood up and went over to his bass and flicked a switch that made the speaker boom then hum. He put on his headphones and plucked his strings silently and swayed to an inaudible rhythm. I lay on the couch, legs hanging over the armrest, and dozed off.

When I woke, he was gone.

My first task was to clean the toilet so I could enter without choking. Then I dealt with the empty blue-furred jam and peanut-butter jars and other remains of food.

In the evening, after dark, I went round to the bar.

That night, after closing the bar, we went back to the attic together and I sat on the sofa and smoked my first joint in quite some time and the dozy medium-sized objects of the material world stepped forward and presented themselves with the clarity of the bed and chair in Van Gogh's bedroom in Arles.

Ritzi, sitting at the porthole window in the director's chair, gripping a little pair of binoculars, whispered urgently:

'Hey! Turn off the light.'

I flicked the switch on the lamp. We were in total darkness.

'Why the whispers, Ritz?' I asked, in a normal voice.

The little pair of binoculars was clamped to his eyes. He spoke in a low, throaty voice: 'She gets in around this time, walks around a bit, strips off. Perfect body, long hair, doesn't have a boyfriend. Walks around like that.'

I went over and took the binoculars from Ritzi. Across the street, one floor below and slightly to the right, was a lighted window.

'Here,' said Ritzi, surrendering his chair. 'You have to sit down and keep it steady or it shakes about too much.'

I sat and looked through and found the lighted window. An empty room.

'Nothing,' I said, almost whispering in the furtive darkness.

'Wait.'

I waited. Then she walked past the window, too suddenly. The angle was wrong and the window too small. She was gone before I could focus.

She appeared a second time. She was a young, slender woman and her hair was tied in a pony-tail. Beyond that, I could not tell much, and she was gone again. The lenses were tricky. Ritzi explained: first you shut your right eye and focused the left, then you closed your left and fine-focused the right. The waiting was a big part of it.

But when the girl did at last appear again she was for one luminous moment vast before my eyes as though projected upon a giant screen and I instinctively held my breath to fix my trembling vision as she untied her hair and shook it out. My eyes were so tired by then I did not know what I saw, only that it was a revelation from another world. There across the street, a girl who worked in a bar or a club, who came home late at night, alone, tired, and removed her make-up.

I passed the binoculars to Ritzi and went back to the couch and sat there in the dark, drinking. Occasionally Ritzi would say something.

'It's happening. She's undressing now.'

And finally: 'That's it. It's over. She's turned the light off.'

I pulled the cord on the lamp. Now lit, the air seemed hazy, as though blurred with glowing reddish dust. Ritzi stood up and stretched. His eyes were bloodshot and the binoculars had imprinted little semicircles beneath each swollen lid. He looked stunned. Like a creature habituated to gloomy depths—underwater or underground—that had been hauled to the surface.

'Ritz, I've got to introduce you to some nice women.'

'You know some?'

I did indeed know some women, really fine people in fact, and some of them were single. But when I thought about them some more, and thought of Ritzi, it no longer looked like a great idea.

In fact, none of my ideas looked like great ideas. I knew Carmen no better than Ritzi knew the girl across the road. She did say all that crazy stuff when we argued late at night, but really she was trying to get at something else. She was trying to get to the fact that I did not love her the way she wanted me to, the way I should have. And I pretended I did not hear what she was saying, and that made me a liar.

What I really loved was my own space, where I did not have to lie.

Now I had all the space I needed. I put a blanket on the floor and lay awake in the dark, eyes open, listening to the roaches clicking and scratching among the papers and upon the dusty wooden floorboards. They were angry because the peanut-butter jars were gone. I thought of them walking on me as I slept. I would have to get some spray in the morning.

I lay there for what felt like a very long time, listening. Then I fell asleep very late in the only city I had ever lived in, and in my dreams found myself living in another city. I believed in its reality while I dreamed, and did not remember the city where I slept. I had a whole past life in my dream city, and complex memories of my time there, of dream-friends and dream-obligations. I had a task to complete, and a destination, and recalled the streets and the interiors of the buildings as I went, new but familiar, as it is when you remind yourself of your own life, which forever runs away from you even as you live it and needs always to be recalled. I followed stairways, passed through the corridors and interconnecting rooms of buildings of extravagant complexity, and in a tiny office found the man who gave me the key. With this key I was to travel across the city to an old house, and that house was entirely empty except for a padlocked trunk—like a pirate's chest with a vaulted top—in the middle of the central room. So I set off again through the streets, because the box contained old reels of film I had shot a long time ago, during the course of my life in the city, and these reels gleamed like treasure in my dream-imagination. These images, edited and composed, would become my masterwork.

And when I woke I did not know where I was. Monsters carried giant boulders over a vast sunlit plain—a line of ants marching before my face, bearing crumbs. The sun shone through the window and hit the dusty floorboards where I lay. Then I understood where I was and what had happened to me. And I was glad the terrible dream city was not real, that I did not have to undergo its trials. My sole regret was I had lost the reels of film I had never shot.

Spring

Business to see to, me and the kid. I rise from the mattress to make the coffee. One pace from pillow to stovetop. Perfect little room. Her bed, my mattress, one next to the other. The table where we eat. Back at Christmas she wanted a tree like everyone else and I jammed it in. Cried when she saw it—it was so small.

She wakes, slips from her bed and pads towards me, arms stretched high, in overlarge red pyjamas with reindeer. She's small for her age. Come here, little monkey. I pick her up and she clings, bed-warm and smelling of sleep. I walk to the window. We are on the seventh floor and the sky grants vast apocalyptic sunsets with locust-swarms of crows, and huge gleaming moons, and for nighttime electric storms we turn off the lights and watch the fireworks in the dark, gripping each other.

Cheeks pressed together, we survey the frozen morning streets under a dirty sky. We're at the peaceful back of the building. All that rages is on the other side. No complaints about the room. But it isn't ours. We have to get out.

Daddy, I had a dream. A little baby was in a basket and he was floating down the river.

No, Piglet, I told you that story before you went asleep.

She thinks for a moment, trying to sort the strata.

Oatmeal cooked slowly with milk, cinnamon, plump raisins. Into the bowl. Honey, running in the heat, a sprinkle of finely chopped walnuts. I watch her eat. I watch every spoonful.

Coffee for me. I don't eat breakfast, but what's left in her bowl, sometimes her dry crusts with a memory of butter and honey.

I'm fifty. She's five.

Not so much left of me.

I clear the dishes, head for the bathroom. When I'm on the toilet she stands at the other side of the door. Not a door. A sliding panel. She asks what I'm doing. My own private business, I say. She knows what that means. I take a shower, she's shouting something. I can't hear over the sound of the water. What? What are you doing now? I'm washing myself! Now what are you doing? I'm drying myself! How long will it take?

Finally, I wrap the towel around me and hunker down by the sliding door at her level, silently. I slide the door back upon its rollers and—surprise!—we're face to face and laughing at each other.

We get dressed. Hats and coats and scarves. Into the lift.

The street—noise and freezing air. Screaming vehicles charging on and off the ramp for the bridge that traverses the railway tracks.

What a shitty town!

And spring is here. Mountain ranges of banked-up snow melt into black sludge. Pedestrians grimace and squelch about the margins of befouled lakes. The first December snowfall sparkled for a day, then drew the poison from the air, was churned by feet and wheels with the dirt on the ground, getting more deeply sullied with each successive partial melt and freeze. Where the thaw is most advanced the footpath is strewn with shit. The reindeer herders in Yakutsk sometimes come across mammoths poking out of the ice. We get constellations of dog turds.

The drivers have no gratitude. What a racket! A faceless quarrel, behind spattered windshields.

Those machines cost hard-earned money, and they pay by the month, so move over, motherfucker—blaaarp!

We're fighting too, me and the kid—no surrender!

Daddy, in our new house can I have a cat?

You bet, Piglet, course you can.

We get the green man and I step from the kerb and swing her over a small sea of icebergs. She likes that. My boots are waterproof up to the ankle. I'm a genius.

We squish onwards, holding hands, across hostile terrain.

She's wearing a brightly coloured woollen hat, bobble-top and earflaps. Nose pink with cold. I lift her aloft to board the tram. Yeah, she's cute in ugly weather. I bear her through public transport like a shield. The crowd parts and we are offered a seat. She perches on my lap and looks out the window. The tracks shunt us down the inner ring road, a monochrome reel of ten-storey apartment blocks, the last gasps of the collectivist utopia. The old Pharaoh had them pouring concrete day and night, and on the Sabbath. He dreamed in concrete. The road girds the capital's heart. Wide enough to tease the traffic with fantasies of speed but choked up anyway.

We get off, stand with the crowd on a narrow pedestrian island. The machines swarm past, too close. Our turn— go! We scuttle across four shiny black lanes. All the snow is reserved for the sides of the roads and the footpaths. Again, at the kerb, I swing the kid over a meltwater lake as the metal beasts start to growl. Some of the less well-shod pedestrians stop before the lake, confused, like cattle on a clifftop, and the lights change—blaaarp!

The estate agent is sipping her skinny cigarette in the street. Her big day too. Three per cent. Her head is a little too big for her frame and it is this imperfection that makes her beauty tangible, like there might be a route through this world to it.

I first met the estate agent on an icy day in January. We stood in the street, outside a modest interwar deco block, reeking of neglect. She was afraid of the dogs in the yard so she telephoned a woman inside with the key. The keyholder came down and escorted us through the miserable little yard. The dogs hung back and snarled. Sacks of refuse piled in an alcove at the bottom of the grimy unlit stairway. Six apartments, two per floor. We walked up to the top and entered the property. The owner had lived there alone for years after the death of his wife. His sons were in America. Then he died too and the place had been empty for over a year. In one room, the plaster was detaching in places from the ceiling and the walls were discoloured with mould. We went up to the attic level via a service stairway to find the source of the leaks. Huge attic-floor—potentially big enough for two apartments. And both the stairway and the garret crammed with junk belonging to the deceased.

It was what I could afford. And it could take a quake. Structurally solid, no cracks.

And you can fix things, can't you?

Back down from the attic, in the apartment again, I instructed myself to think of the light through the south-facing windows one day in summer and composed other legends of my victorious future self. I pulled the yellowed curtains aside to maximise the light. The estate agent smiled at me and I smiled back at her.

She finishes her little cigarette. Up to the fifth floor, the three of us. Desires a child herself, she says, maybe they'd try soon. Oh, so she's married. All along I thought she'd been flirting.

Bright office, cheap new furniture. A woman who will sign for the sons in America is already waiting for us.

I give the kid paper and colouring pencils from my backpack. While the contract is prepared she draws our new home, sectioned, the way you see the interiors of bombed-out or half-demolished buildings. Egyptian cartoon strip. Rooms as squares. Bathroom, bedrooms, living room, kitchen. Me and her—and a cat—living our pastel lives. I scan the old deeds, yellow parchment, a transaction, 1941, Coppel, German name, no, Jewish. This was the Jewish quarter. March 8… Weeks after the pogrom. A mob, shops ransacked, basement torture chambers, corpses hanging from meat-hooks. Immediately I'm filling in the blanks, somebody with sense, Jewish, emigrating, selling cheap to a young couple, their friends, Betty and Nathan. I read on. Betty and Nathan sell up in 1950—the commies are on their way and the Jews that haven't been killed are getting out. Someone else will come and fill their homes. There's another transaction and then the recently dead guy turns up in 1983.

We all think we're the last and most important.

The women are talking to the kid. She's opening up.

I'm going to have a kitten. Her name will be Mitzi.

The notary brings the contract. Snow-white paper beside the old sepia deeds with their clunky type-font. My signature. Then down the slushy street to the bank. Electronic sorcery. Keys in hand.

Just me and the kid again. Another tram. Away from the monster boulevard, towards the centre. Uniformity cedes to a jumble of smaller, older buildings. Chunks of decorative façade and plaster crumbling away in merry patterns, as though demons, gremlins, emerge nightly with hammers and chisels and hack at anything integral. The attempts to patch things up add variety to the decadence. Wooden window-frames mutate to white plastic. Black cables spiderweb from lampposts and rooftops, lacing the air. An accretion of commercial signage offers mobile telephony and relief from prostate problems. The pools of meltwater from the sudden thaw make it look like a city in the wake of a disaster, or struck by some plague or curse— the healthy evacuated, a demoralised remnant population dragging itself through the ruins.

Our stop. A crossroads. A gentle rain now stipples the puddles and greys the air. A supermarket, a couple of betting shops, pharmacies, a pawnbroker's and kiosks selling magazines and flowers. On one corner the towering concrete skeleton of an abandoned construction project.

We cross the road to a once-inhabited building on another corner, its bricked-up doors and windows covered with posters for concerts and revues featuring heavily made-up middle-aged women in festive peasant costume.

Round a corner, a quieter street. Our little yard, where the snow is half-melted. No sign of the dogs. They seem to mostly keep to the back, behind the block. We ascend the stairwell, light through dirty lead-framed frosted windows from a deep, narrow, inner courtyard. Some of the windows are cracked, broken, others repaired with rectangles of translucent plastic. All this was beautiful once, I tell myself as we ascend, and will be again. The curving stairway, the curving black bannister, and walls that will be white.

The steps are wet. I hear drips. The water is dripping from the stairwell ceiling. The thaw? I try my new key in the lock and my door opens.

It's big! she says, skipping like a little goat straight into the room she has guessed is hers. Yes, in the entrance hall you can stretch out your arms and not touch the walls. A room for her and a room for me. She's opening the rickety door to her little balcony, undeterred by the grime and junk, but I don't hear what she's asking me. I'm staring at the bathroom wall, down which a small waterfall is flowing. The entire bathroom ceiling is wet and dripping. Rivulets trickle down the wall in the hall too. The plasterwork above me, in poor shape to begin with, is now ready to detach in wet clumps from wide areas of the ceiling. The kid's new room, where it borders the bathroom, is also leaking from above, and water is pooling on the parquet. She's just run through a puddle and left wet tracks. The old oak floor has no varnish left and is slowly drinking it up. Soon the walls will turn to mush and the old electrics will fizzle and pop.

Just a moment, Piglet.

The door to the secret stairway opens from the kitchen. It ascends parallel to the official stairway, separated by a wall. I enter the junkyard. The kid follows. Once upon a time, before the war, each apartment had a servant and this was the way to their quarters in the garret. Improvised cupboards have been built, blocking out the light from the windows to the yard. Bags are tied to the bannisters. I distinguish boxes, broken chairs, a bicycle wheel, but mostly the objects have settled together in a dust-fuzzed, amorphous heap. Now the attic. A dripping skylight, missing a pane, a drift of snow beneath it. At the end of the passage, light shining through a broken doorway from an open terrace. A stream can be heard tinkling somewhere among the detritus and I have to reach the source. For decades people have parked their things here and then left this world. I reach for a huge black plastic bag and it rises, supernaturally, like a helium balloon. At some point the dead guy stopped throwing plastic bottles out. Saved them for later. The kid's eyes shine with wonder. I fight through the treasure, shifting aside a giant television aerial, a fridge, drawers filled with electronic components and a sodden cardboard box that splits open, spewing old Russian textbooks. *Tehnicheskii* this and that. Finally, an old metal sink, a tap. I notice now, in the corner, a toilet and a cistern, pipes... A bathroom, for the servants... The tap is releasing a trickle of water, and beneath the sink the drainage pipe is broken. The junk has sponged up all it can and now it's percolating down. The attic exposed to the weather, the water must have frozen in the winter, damaged the tap. I give the spigot a twist to close the water off but something breaks. The water whooshes out, unstoppable...

Daddy, is this a flood?

Yes, Pork-pie. It is a flood.

Hurry, through eons of junk, down the service stairway, to the ground floor. Junkroom dungeons, ancient pipes snake along the ceiling. Nowhere to turn off the water. The kid appears beside me. Had forgotten about her for a second. Seldom happens.

Back upstairs. I find a twenty-litre plastic canister and hold it to the tap. With my free hand I pull my crappy old telephone from my pocket. My sight has deteriorated in recent years and the screen is blurred. This feeling of blindness and things breaking in my hand and working against the clock is one of my standard dreams. Or premonitions. Well, things do fall apart. You were warned. I call the plumber, leave a recorded message. The battery on my phone is low. The canister is now full. I carry it down the hallway and out through the open doorway. On the terrace is a door, broken glass and other objects I can't identify under a drift of compacted snow. Most of the snow has melted and the exposed surface is fissured. The source of my long-term leaks. A generous space, two metres wide, running along the front of the building. Perhaps the servants had hung the laundry here. Or drank wine under the stars. I empty the canister into a drain. As I straighten up and turn to go back in I see it, past naked trees and over the tops of buildings, three kilometres away, unimpressive in the hazy air, an aborted ziggurat, the Pharaoh's palace.

I fill and empty the canister. Twenty minutes. Half an hour. The kid pokes about in the attic, exploring. She emerges from shadows from time to time to peer at me. The plumber isn't calling back and the phone will die when he does.

This is no good, Piglet. We need help.

Down the service stairs one flight, through my kitchen, down the official stairway two floors. Mrs Gurau, the keyholder I met that day, answers the door, smiling, So you bought it, and is this your little girl? Yes, yes, but but but! No, she doesn't know where to turn off the water, doesn't know a plumber. In this block only widows and crazies, she says. She follows me back up, alerting another neighbour on the way, a very old woman, who gets on the phone.

I'm back to collecting the surging water and sending it down the drain on the terrace, down a rusted drainpipe. I suspect this just inundates my apartment at a different point. But I can't believe my actions are futile. The kid is watching me.

Daddy, my feet are cold.

Try not walking through the water, Pork-chop.

Why are we doing this?

So the roof of our home doesn't collapse.

What does collapse mean?

To break, to fall in, to disintegrate into a lot of tiny pieces.

If it does, all this rubbish will fall into our house, won't it?

We laugh. I dump another canister of water on the terrace. I resume my post at the tap.

Daddy, I'm hungry.

What will we eat? Something hot!

Pizza!

I'm hungry too, but I keep baling. Another canister, and another.

Daddy, I'm cold.

Your feet are cold?

All of me is.

The flow of water becomes a slim thread, ceases entirely. I put the canister down. My arms are tired and the joints at the elbow hurt. Footsteps on the stairs. Mrs Gurau and a neighbour from one of the houses at the back, where the dogs hang out. He nods at me curtly, looks around at the disorder, disapproves of something, everything. Then he's gone. Mrs Gurau explains. The neighbour has turned off the water for the whole block and the houses at the back. A plumber has been called.

Back later, I say. Got to feed this kid.

The street, slushy footpaths. Wind in our eyes, her icy hand in mine. Afternoon now and at the playschool they'd be putting her down for her nap. She's cold, begins to whimper. I scoop her up, support her with my left arm and unzip my coat at the neck. She slips her hands under my scarf, against my skin. She tucks her face in and settles there, resting. I put my right arm around her shoulders. I know a place, fifteen minutes at most, walking.

A narrow, tree-lined, residential street. The houses are old, but decently maintained. The restaurant is a converted townhouse. I set the kid on her feet and push the door and a bell jingles. There is a tank with tropical fish in the little entrance hallway. Wooden tables, a smell of fried garlic, seafood, steam. We sit down, unburden ourselves of hats, coats, scarves. Her nose is red and her hair tousled from her hat. I sit her in my lap and take off her boots so that she can sit comfortably with her legs under her. Her socks are wet.

We made it, Piglet. Sit down there.

I'm tired from carrying her through the cold streets, slowly, negotiating the slick icy patches. I haven't eaten all day. And this is good, this warm place, and the low mumble from the television on the other side of the room and over the counter the glow from the pizza oven, real fire, logs. And tacky pictures of the Colosseum and Capri, and a still from a black and white 1950s movie, looks like a comedy, a fat guy with a paper bib eating spaghetti. Another still, a man and a little boy, *The Bicycle Thieves*, it's after the war, in Rome, they're desperate, starving, and he has to get his bicycle back or he's out of a job, he has a wife and kid, and the kid follows him around the city, but how could he imagine he would ever get the bicycle back? At the end of this ordeal the man sees an unattended bicycle, paces back and forth, tells the boy to take a tram home. Just as he grabs the bike the owner appears. You see him stupidly veer uphill, gravity against him, he doesn't get far, he's seized and the crowd are about to rip him apart, and the little boy runs up and flings himself on the father, crying, Papa!—the kid missed the tram and has seen the whole thing—and the owner of the bicycle decides not to call a policeman. This man has enough trouble, he says. And in this moment of mercy you hear the hint of a morality that might save the world. The crowd dissipates. The stunned and humiliated father slowly walks away with the boy. They are holding hands, and the boy looks up at his father, who is looking ahead, trying not to weep. Someone shouts, You should be ashamed of yourself!

The end.

I was younger, nobody needed me, didn't care where I slept. Woke in a cell once and didn't mind much.

The waiter brings the menu and without looking at it I order a glass of red wine and a glass of freshly squeezed orange juice.

Come here, Piglet, let's get these off you.

I peel off the damp socks and throw them in my little backpack. Then I lift her towards me and she stands on my thighs, facing me, holding on to my shoulders. I gently massage her cold feet and toes until they're dry.

I rummage in the backpack, past property deeds, contracts, electronic-transfer statements. I find a pair of socks, rolled into a neat bundle. The socks I put there that morning. I unroll the clean dry socks and put them on her feet. Thick socks, good socks. They are pink and have little rabbits on them. There is satisfaction in these small important things I can do right. The waiter brings the drinks. I order food and he leaves. I put her back on her own chair, kneeling so that she can reach over the table more easily. Plastic straw. She likes that. She drinks the juice nearly to the end. She is reviving in the warmth of this more hospitable environment.

We clink glasses.

I feel the drink hit my empty belly.

We did a great thing today, Pork-Chop.

Our new house is broken and it's dirty.

Yes. Yes. But. Every day we can do something to make it better. And you'll start school. And you can have a cat. And your own room.

Is that bed going to be my bed?

The dead guy's bed is made of chipboard, drawers underneath containing his clothes, and some of his wife's clothes too, in plastic bags, mothballed. All the furniture is laminated chipboard or plywood, from the land where the craftsmen were exiled to the factory. The bulky chipboard bed is impossibly heavy—I'll have to kick it to pieces. The apartment is weighed down with past lives.

I'll get you a new bed.

But what about the flood, Daddy?

That's nothing, Piglet. That means everything's getting better starting now.

I take another swig of wine. I haven't slept properly for about five years but the lighting here is gentle. The one window to the street has been discreetly renovated away. The city no longer exists. Sometimes, lying next to her at night, her bedtime story puts you asleep and you hear her voice, Then what happened? And you remember, the Big Bad Wolf has just blown down the house made out of sticks. You read her the Bible too sometimes, she likes the crazy language and the magic and you both get terribly involved in Exodus. You know the Chosen People will be allowed go in the end but it is going to take some time. Until then, you drink too much, fall asleep on her bed, wake, can't fall asleep again, and then it's another day.

The food comes. Pizza for the kid. For me, seafood stew— mussels, prawns, octopus, unclean invertebrates that draw their flavour filtering and scavenging the rottenness of the sea, and a nice chunk of tuna, and a sauce made of wine and garlic and tomato and cream. The kid munches her margarita and passes the crusts ceremoniously to me. I dip them in the rich warm sauce. I eat, look at her eating hungrily, take swigs of wine until it's gone.

Yes, we did a great thing, Piglet.

I can't tell what's best; eating here with her, or owning real estate, or my self-congratulation at the socks.

It's not so bad, the street again. The light is already ebbing. The day has been too much, even for the day. It can't abide its own mediocrity. It's had it, goodbye. I hoist her up again. These socks will remain dry, relatively, maybe. After the respite, food in my belly, the glow of the wine, she is compact and weightless and I move surefooted over the ever-freer footpaths. We glide back to our new home.

As I open the gate to the yard, a man is emerging from a hole in the ground. His head appears, then his shoulders, and he hoists himself out. I put the kid down. The dismal dusky little yard is dotted with dogshit, black against the half-melted snow. This is the where the mutts do it. There they are, at the back of the building, poking their scraggy heads around the corner, cowardly storybook wolves, growling. The kid hides behind me, holding my coat. The man wheezes, gets from his knees to his feet, hitches up his baggy denims, looks at us. I'm the owner of the flooded apartment, I tell him. Oh, so you're the one? Probably he's been wondering who is going to pay him, what squabbles he will have to sit through. He stands there beside the open manhole, hands on hips, catching his breath. He's not so young, looks part of the building, as though he has been fixing, tweaking, bandaging its eccentricities for quite some time. Instantly I feel an affinity with him. He reminds me of the peculiar independent men in the country where I grew up who drank tea from big dirty mugs and smelled of cattle and didn't care what anybody thought of them. They owned their land and they were kings. This is Victor. He has plugged the pipe in the attic. Straightforward job, last in a series up there. Wrestling decay is his hobby.

Victor got the place habitable for me. Soon we addressed each other casually, using *tu* rather than *Dumneavoastră*, which takes a long time to say and is polite but can cover up much suspicion and aggression. Maybe he wasn't a king, but those old boys back home weren't really either. He mumbled and didn't look you in the eye, his prices were vague, they evolved as the job went on and you were never certain you'd understood each other, or else he would suddenly seize the initiative and do work you hadn't discussed. But he knew the mysteries of the building. He replaced rusted rotten pipes, installed a new bath and toilet and did many other things. It wasn't always perfect; he put in the new radiator upside-down on the bathroom wall and arranged the copper pipes in such a screwy configuration it looked like a modern-art installation, but in the end I liked it. We'd drink beers when he finished and he'd tell me stories about the old people in the building. He knew the lore of the place right back to the two Jewish brothers who had built it and lived there themselves until they fled. He played the trumpet and drove an old turquoise Trabant he maintained in impeccable condition, in contrast to the stained and ill-fitting old clothes he wore. He'd forget to charge his phone and you wouldn't get him for days on end. One day in late spring I needed something done and he wasn't answering and I knew he had a workshop nearby. He'd said he had an apartment in a block in the suburbs, in Berceni, had a wife, but I'd sometimes seen the Trabant parked in front of a building several streets down from mine so I went down to see if the workshop was there. It was warm, the trees mad with change. Winter, decay choked you, then the sun rose a little higher above the rooftops and proclaimed the immanence of the promised earthly paradise. I saw a crazy guy kneeling on the footpath, behind a parked car, praying. I detoured the car, into the road, to leave him undisturbed. When I looked back, I saw he was injecting himself in the neck. I'd had to warn the kid to not touch the needles the sick people left abandoned. Then I heard the trumpet, cutting through the Sunday air, and saw the parked Trabant. I won't say he played perfectly, but I did not want to interrupt, so I waited on the footpath as the notes rose over the hedge and the wooden fence. Behind, through the greenery, was an old house with a porch with columns and a lot of neoclassical flim-flam coming off in chunks. Was Victor heir to a mansion? There were great cracks in the exposed brickwork and it would come down in the next quake. Easier to demolish than to render safe. He was playing 'Amazing Grace'. I knew the melody but not the words. *Amazing Grace, How sweet the sound...* I don't know the rest. When he finished his slave-song I waited a few beats then pushed the gate and went in. He was standing on the stone porch of the house, the steps of a ruined temple, under a sky of unbelievable blue, shaking the spit from his horn. I was afraid I had intruded. I couldn't tell from his face if I had. We shook hands and went into the garage, a wooden shed in the yard beside the house. Three metres wide at the entrance and six or seven deep. We sat on stools and he flicked the switch on an electric kettle to make us tea. The doors were wide open onto the overgrown garden where all these birds were going crazy in the rising heat. The wastepaper basket overflowed with plastic wrappers—chocolate bars and cakes. He had a hot plate and a small fridge. Metal filing cabinets and shelves with parts and pieces, tools and saws and drills, a stack of tyres. You couldn't move with the junk, piled to the ceiling. Furniture, scrap metal, broken fridges and televisions, lumber, old doors and window-frames. Boxes and sacks. Some people had gold in the bank, this pirate had raided the collapsing city and stashed his cave with plunder. You wouldn't have thought he lived there except for the camp bed along one wall. I don't know if he was estranged from his wife in some painful sense or if this was a more comfortable arrangement for the warmer months. You couldn't play a trumpet from the balcony of a block in Berceni without the neighbours screaming obscenities and the cops banging on the door. So I just looked at the camp-bed and wondered. The way people see me with the kid, maybe, and wonder is the mother dead of a rare disease or else trading verses with her lover on the far side of town.

There was a tap and a sink but I don't know how he managed for toilet facilities. He managed. Did I say they weren't kings, those men? Sure they were.

Then I didn't see him for a while. His phone said the person I was calling was unavailable and his gate was locked when I tried. One of the old ladies in my block told me he was in hospital for tests and one hot summer day I looked through the windshield of his turquoise Trabant and saw a handwritten note on the dash:

ABANDONED CAR—OWNER DECEASED

But now he's coming out of the ground.

So, you're the one?

Yes. I'm going to pay.

I cut through the pipe up there and plugged it.

Thank you.

He pushes the manhole cover with his foot. It scrapes then falls into place—clungggk!

It is no great science he engages in. But it is competence at the level we need. Like raising a child—you don't know much, but maybe enough to get you through the season.

And who's this? he asks, looking at the kid.

This is Piglet, I say, except I say her real name.

She's hiding behind me, holding my leg, peeking around at him. She has never seen a person crawl out of a hole like that before, like an animal. The wolves hang back, dark smudges, snarling. Whatever armies are chasing us have been delayed.

Victor wipes his hands on his trousers.

Everything's fine now, he says. The water is back on.

The Book of Love

I was staring out through the plate-glass restaurant window at pensioners bearing cargoes of purchases and a young thug swearing into his phone, and a millionaire was telling me about the importance of cunnilingus. The air was cool where we sat, and the traffic in the raging boulevard outside was muted and you could comfortably observe the pedestrians getting their brains baked. Sol was past sixty and on the wrong side of the Atlantic and he paid women to let him eat them out, because he liked to give pleasure. To taste the sweetness, as he put it. He began by massaging them and did that for up to thirty minutes. He had magic hands, he said.

The waiter came with the coffee for Sol and the beer and vodka shot for me. I drank the vodka immediately.

Sol extended his hands above the table for me to see, showing me the palms and then the backs. The fingers were not long but they were well-formed and the nails manicured and glossy. Delicate hands for such a short, heavy man. He huffed when hurrying to cross a street or squeezing into the back of a cab but otherwise he carried his bulk gracefully.

'I could have been an acupuncturist or physiotherapist. I know all the pressure points. Mental tension knots the muscle. We jam problems in our flesh and they stick there like memories. I feel those points straight off. When we were kids, in Jersey, me and my brother would stretch out on the sofa and take turns giving each other foot massages. He's a neurologist now, on Oahu. Has his own chopper. He gets around the islands on it.'

He ripped open three sachets of brown sugar and sprinkled them onto his cappuccino. The granules lay upon the bed of foam, darkening.

'When they're ready, I go to work with my tongue. I don't enter a woman until they come at least once. A woman doesn't need a big penis to get off. Mine's not big. A bit on the small side, actually, in terms of length. In thickness, pretty much the regular size, I think. It's how you move it. And patience. Most men have no patience.'

My phone rang. I checked the name. My business partner, eager to know if the deal had gone through. It hadn't. I rejected the call.

'I know it's not my looks. Women like tall men and I'm not tall.'

Stature was the least of it. I was fascinated by the topography of his great bald head, how the bumps and ridges about the forehead and temples caught the light and shifted as he spoke. It was an animal head. A project for a sculptor. But these girls came willingly, eagerly, he said, and brought their friends along too sometimes.

'We're talking prostitutes here, right?'

'I support them, yes. But it's nice. We hang out. You know, I don't pay by the hour. They get their monthly allowance. But they call me up and come round to get laid properly, because I'm nice to them.'

'Five of them, you say?'

'That I support steadily, yes.'

'And others?'

'Not steadily, those.'

There were morning and evening visits and often one in the afternoon. He varied the routine only if something intervened.

'I hope I'm not keeping you.'

He dismissed this idea with a wave of his hand.

My phone rang again. My wife didn't like me working on Saturdays. I excused myself and stepped out of the restaurant. The heat was terrible. The roar from the traffic was no good either. She wanted me to bring her ice cream. Also, maybe she was going into labour.

'I had a pain. But it was about an hour ago.'

'Is it starting?'

'I don't know. I don't think so. I don't know how it's supposed to feel.'

'Call me if it happens again.'

'How long will you be?'

'I'm winding something up.'

I promised not to forget the ice cream then I called my partner. Sol had been looking at a share in a residential development on the outskirts—a gated community with its own retail and sports facilities and swimming pool. People could leave their jobs behind, drive out of the stink and heat and noise of the city, and when they got home they could pretend they were in America. I told my partner there was no deal, we were having a friendly drink, and perhaps there'd be a next time. We had the one car between us, for appearances, and even that was getting ridiculous. Back in the boom it was easy to feel like a business genius but there was no room now in the market for small operators. I could hear his kids in the background, fighting, and then a woman's voice crying his name over the noise. The vehicles shimmered and wobbled in the heat.

I went back inside and sat down.

'My wife. We're expecting our first. At any moment.'

'Boy or girl?'

'Boy.'

'Congratulations. My son's an idiot. Blew the pile he inherited from his stepfather. Wouldn't listen to me. Like he wants to fail. I have no other explanation. When my wife was pregnant I pleaded with her to have an abortion. I begged her.'

'Must have liked that story. Your son.'

'Never told him. Not until he was a man himself.'

'Still.'

'You never discussed an abortion, you and your wife?'

I shook my head.

She had had two miscarriages. Her friends, her sister, everybody was having kids. Babies every time you stepped out onto the street. The one thing anybody could do. We are both thirty-nine years old.

The waiter came with a joint of lamb for Sol and a Pizza Siciliana for me. I ordered more beer and vodka. Sol produced a jar from his little leather satchel and pursed his lips primly as he spooned a glob of green jelly onto the lamb.

'Mint sauce. Can't get this stuff here. I brought it from England.'

I sprinkled chilli flakes on my pizza. We began to eat. After the vodka and beer I was very hungry.

'My first wife—this was back in the seventies when we were crazy to liberate ourselves—she confessed one day she wanted nothing more than a cock in both fists. We were smoking weed, the kid was a few years old, and our neighbour Larry used to come round regularly. Good-looking young guy. Not that I was interested in Larry. I don't swing that way. My wife was the meat in the sandwich. Then we were getting divorced and she wanted to keep seeing Larry. Imagine how Larry felt about that— crazy divorced woman with a kid! Suddenly you didn't see Larry much around the neighbourhood. After the divorce, just to get me pissed, she says, You know, when we were married I'd meet Larry at night, just the two of us, and we'd fuck on the golf course. I said, Keep talking, baby! You're getting me horny!'

He paused and speared more lamb.

'People get married thinking they'll nail happiness. Well, not a nailable commodity. They should have these guys with trumpets like in the Middle Ages. Whattaya call 'em—heralds? Town criers? "Stop trying to nail happiness!" Let them cry that. Another person happening along and rectifying the craziness in your skull? The odds are stacked. After the divorce I went out to the West Coast and started on the psychedelics—psilocybin and mescaline and acid. But the first time I took mushrooms was down in Mexico, and I had this vision of myself, a train moving down these dark tracks, in a tunnel, gloomily, to my death, ignorant, while whole universes exploded either side of me. It woke me up. Until then I was a robot. They sent me to school, in

Trenton, New Jersey, I went out into the world and made some cash, I produced a son. That trip I was blasted apart. Then I found myself on the board of the Albert Hofmann Foundation. Know who Albert Hofmann was?'

'The man who invented LSD?'

'Discovered, you might say. Synthesised.'

'You knew Hofmann?'

My drinks arrived.

'The Foundation was named in Hofmann's honour—this was out in LA and Hofmann wasn't personally involved. But yes, as a matter of fact, I did meet Albert once. In Switzerland. He was very old. We met at his house and had coffee and cakes. A very nice old German gentleman. Well, Swiss—I shouldn't call him German. He came out onto his porch to greet me and he took my hands in his. He said, you have beautiful hands, Herr Sol. He could sense there was something special in my hands. I'd never seen it myself until then. Tears were running down my cheeks and I didn't even feel embarrassed. My own father had never said to me a thing so decent. It was like he was blessing me. So he's holding my hands and smiling, and here I am, this fat slob from New Jersey, biting my lip, getting choked up. I was just an idiot who got on the board of the Foundation because I gave them money. A few tens of thousands at a time, not as much as Donald would have liked—Don was the director. And here I was meeting this saint. People tell these stories about the Dalai Lama. Albert had that sort of kindness and I'm not surprised he lived a century. He was pure sugar, that man. Timmy Leary was not like that. Loudmouthed Irishman. It was all legal until he started his shenanigans. Then off to Algeria with the Black Panthers.

Nixon called him the most dangerous man in America. Gotta love a guy gets that reaction. But he did more to harm the serious research of psychedelics than anybody. Me and Don would be up there begging him to keep his mouth shut.'

'You knew Leary too?'

'I was in charge of the nitrous oxide machine at his farewell bash. Timmy was sick then. Prostate cancer. We were having his birthday send-off at his pad, up in the hills. He ended up blasted into outer space. His ashes. On a rocket. Along with a load of other famous people. Nobel scientists and so on. Gene Roddenberry, too. Never heard of Gene Roddenberry? Created *Star Trek*! The original series. Kirk and Spock? They were Jews, both of them, the two top guys in space. Love it. The actors, I mean. Shatner and Nimoy. The one with the pointy ears was Nimoy. So there's Timmy with a few months to live, but he can't stop showing off and talking and partying. And I was manning the nitrous oxide machine at the send-off.'

'This is the gas dentists use?'

'But a recreational drug a century before it had any surgical application. Timmy didn't want morphine for the pain. Had his prejudices on the subject of opiates. So he got in a good stock of gas. Filled little balloons. You'd call by and it was like a kid's birthday party, him lying in bed dying, inhaling from these coloured balloons, tripping into the next dimension. "Taking the factitious airs," that's what he called it.'

'Factitious airs?'

'Right—blarney! Anyway, hundreds of people there the night of the goodbye party, and I'm by the pool, in charge of the machine. There's a queue of people. I deal hits and take hits and when it gets too much I delegate, I pass out, I pass over, but I go until dawn working the machine. I was inhabiting the vision. A liberating vision, of my own nothingness. I was very depressed after my second divorce, and then, whoosh, suddenly I could put things in perspective, intellectually. You know the story of Indra and the ants? You know the Upanishads?'

I confessed I didn't. Sol wiped his chin with a paper napkin and looked at the silent gleaming vehicles as they passed down the boulevard. He put the napkin on the plate beside the bone.

'Then let me tell you. This is very important. It was a time of drought and chaos throughout the world. A demon was sucking life from the earth by drying out rivers and springs. Crops were withering and deserts were expanding. Wars were breaking out between states over resources, and within states between factions. Until this god called Indra discovered he had a box of thunderbolts. Hurled them at the demon and killed him, and the waters flowed again and the land was fertile and people were happy. What a clever kid I am, said Indra, and to celebrate his achievement he built a palace atop the highest mountain. He got the craftsman god, Vishwakarma, to do his building for him. Indra did what any talented, ambitious being does; he strove for grandness and perfection. He created the most beautiful palace on Earth. And then he came back and added more. Another wing, another level, another balcony looking over another pleasure garden, another degree of detailed decoration on the columns of another hall. There was no end to Indra's desire for expansion and perfection and Vishwkarma was exhausted. Oh shit! thought Vishwakarma. We're immortal, so this is going to take forever…'

'This is the vision you have working Leary's gas machine…'

'I saw myself as the slave of my life of trouble, a hamster spinning on its wheel. It was the awakening in me of wisdom. If you were immortal, what would you work at? Wouldn't your most inspired project become an endless task? And so I had the vision of my death, or rather the meaningfulness of my death, and the meaninglessness of all the suffering I had brought upon myself. So I get one of these machines rigged up at home and arrange things so I can inhabit my vision pretty much most of the time. My dream. Don't look down on dreams. People present themselves prosaically, but don't you believe it. People aren't rational. What about all those people driving around in cars out there? If people were rational they'd stay in one place. There'd be no need for moving. And don't tell me capitalism creates the desire for the gadgets and the machines. You've had dreams where you fly, where you run effortlessly, where you whizz through landscapes, right? So did cavemen. This dream of liberation from the limitations of the body. And all this travelling in machines, in trains and planes and automobiles, is the fulfilment of the desire to see the world as it has always been seen. It's actively entering the dream state. The whole world wants it, burning the resources of the entire planet to realise the collective dream. Well, I didn't buy a car. I had another dream, one that showed me the unreality of the dream I'd been inhabiting previously. Just like Indra building his palace. I was malnourished eventually. I had sores all over my legs.'

'After Leary's party?'

'Not after the party! I was tripping for over a year, in my apartment. Then I was in the hospital. There's nothing harmful about nitrous oxide, chemically, but you do start to neglect yourself. I'd take my trash out to the chute but in my vision it was a *prasad*, an offering to the gods. A couple of times I locked myself out, naked, on these trips to the temple—and that was awkward. But what finished it for me was finally *I* was the offering to the gods. Yes, I ended up sending *myself* down the trash chute from four floors up in my condo. Don't look so surprised. I wasn't so fat then. But still it was a squeeze. In my mind I was flying back to my home planet where the atmosphere was pure nitrous oxide, not the corrupt mix of nitrogen and oxygen we breathe here, but in reality I was just wiggling down the trash chute. When I came to, I was bruised and I thought I was turning blue, turning into Vishnu. In the dumpster, naked, swimming in garbage. That's where the super found me. Then they took me away. And I laid off the gas and recovered my health. When I started in again it was with ketamine, three times a day. And that went on for four years. That's about four thousand hits. No clinical record of such a thing, anywhere, according to my brother. I'm a scientific wonder.'

Sol was wearing a short-sleeved shirt. He noticed me looking at his arms.

'Hey, it's not smack. You don't mainline. Intramuscular. Very fine needle. Mosquito bite. Once a year I'd cross over to Tijuana with this guy. He'd get a litre, almost, of K, from a veterinary wholesaler. Then drop the bag at the door of my hotel room. I'd put it in a litre tequila bottle so it looked like I'd just opened it and taken a slug. We'd cross back over the border separately. I'd have an unopened bottle of tequila with me and an almost full bottle of K—my legal tax-free allowance. Enough to last almost a year.'

'So you were addicted to this stuff?'

'It's not addictive. A dissociative anaesthetic. Like the nitrous oxide. Mind and body go their separate ways. You trip. And I was going back to the same dream. I didn't finish the story, about Indra. This is important.'

'Go on.'

'What happens is that Vishwakarma gets tired being Indra's builder, so he goes to Vishnu for help.'

'I don't know anything about the hierarchy of these deities.'

'Vishnu is God. Indra is just *a* god, and though he has some supernatural ability he inhabits history and has trouble seeing beyond it. Just like you and me.'

'Okay.'

'So Vishnu turns up at the palace in the form of a small boy, and Indra invites him in and shows him around. At one point the boy sees a line of ants walking across the floor of the palace and starts laughing. What are you laughing at? asks Indra. I'm laughing, says the boy, because every one of those ants was an Indra who built a palace. Each one dropped a thunderbolt and thought, what a clever kid I am.

'Then it hits Indra that he is blind, that he is repeated to infinity, that the facets of infinity reflect endless variants of Indra, that the work of building makes sense only when you're trapped in a tight little corner, like an ant moving a grain of sand on the shore of the sea of time. The building came to an end. No more palaces for Indra. Something else about Vishnu. He is the sleeping god. Vishnu is asleep on the cosmic ocean. A lotus grows from his belly, and Brahma the creator god sits on the lotus, and when Brahma opens his eyes a universe comes into being, and endures for hundreds of thousands of years, and then another lotus appears and another Brahma and he opens his eyes, and so universes appear and disappear, and they all have their Indras, all flowing from Vishnu's dream, and Brahma's fertility, and all the Indras on all their missions, walking across the palace floor.

'So Indra, disillusioned, falls into a slump. He dismisses his builder and heads into the forest to contemplate. But he has a beautiful queen called Indrani, and Indrani lodges a complaint with the authorities. Something in the order of "What about *my* needs?" So a divine counselling session is held and the priest of the gods sets Indra straight. Listen, Indra, he says. You inhabit history. There's nothing wrong with your place in the cosmos. Deal with it. Be a decent deity and don't get carried away. And I'm going to write a manual for you kids called *The Book of Love* so that you know that in uniting you are participating in the mystery of creation. Now, scram!'

I caught the waiter's eye and indicated my empty glasses.

'Is that when you started eating pussy?'

'Ha! Very funny! I devoted my tongue to the rosebud much later in my spiritual journey. I was telling you about the ketamine episode. I was neglecting my nutrition again. If I'd been smart I would have organised that side of things better—vitamin supplements and so on. See that tooth? Not real. One morning I just spat it out, and I noticed the rest were kind of wobbly. I had sense enough to realise this was not good but when I went down to the dentist for a new tooth I told him, Don't give me nitrous oxide, I don't touch it these days. I took out my own needle and a hit of K. He says, Okay, Sol, come back tomorrow, I'll give you a tooth. This guy is an old friend of my brother's and early next morning there's a knock on the door and guess who's just flown in from Hawaii? Hello, I say. What are you doing here? And we sit down and I tell my brother about Indra and Indrani, just like I'm telling you, and he listens and nods his head. Like okay, whatever, you fruitcake. I wake up in a clinic in Oahu and I can see the ocean outside and brightly coloured birds flitting between the trees. Very nice place. Private room. Big windows. The doctors give me different drugs for a nice easy landing. All very professional. Was I allowed leave? No idea. I was happy lying there, looking at the ocean, and it was a couple of months before they suggested it was time I move along. Then I thought I might as well do something with my money. In the years I'd been high my investments did well. I had a few million.'

'You got rich while tripping?'

'Probably before. Modest investments. A flashy lifestyle doesn't interest me.'

The waiter brought me another vodka and beer.

'I needed an occupation and that's when I became particularly interested in women. Actually, it was partly Castaneda's fault I'd put it off—'

'Wait a minute. Carlos Castaneda?'

'We'd tripped a few times, way back in the eighties, in

my pre-dissociative-anaesthetic phase, when I just did psychedelics. He called me Sunshine. Sol means 'sun' in Spanish, see? A very charming man, very funny. A Californian psychedelic shaman, and this is the period after my train of desolation experience. I'd been blind to the world and had opened my eyes and there was Carlos, to tell me what it meant. If Carlos liked you, he'd hold your hand, so-to-speak, and tell you the stuff Don Juan told him. There I was, stepping out of the darkness, and Carlos is calling me Sunshine. Later on Carlos was living in a big house in LA in secret with a load of women and it got a bit creepy because I think they all disappeared after he died, just walked into the desert to meet whatever miracle he told them was waiting there. Got fried by the sun probably, poor things. But back in the mid-eighties he was investigating the sacramental dimension of sexuality. He gave me peyotl and turned three women loose on me. They were changing shape, going from women to wolverines and back again. After what felt like a week being fucked by cats I came out of it and decided I was through with drugs. Took a long break from women, too. But after the ketamine, I realised what was missing. Indra had been neglecting Indrani. I set out to study *The Book of Love*. I thought, what country has a nice climate and beautiful women? So I headed down to Costa Rica and started looking at some property. And I had lots of sex and didn't mind paying. Buying up tracts of the interior. Thousands of hectares of virgin land. I'm not developing it. It's where I'm going to go when the shit hits.'

I asked what he meant.

'Ecological disaster. Global warming. Rising oceans. Or

the coming wars. We like to think the big ones are behind us. In the barbaric past. And why should that be, tell me please? Babylon thought it had it made. A bit of irrigation. The miracle of wheat and the sweet settled life. Environmental disasters will bring on social collapse. Populations are expanding, states competing for declining resources. See how angry the Arabs are? Can't be otherwise. Their religion is young. They're caught up in history. Adolescents, just setting out, and they know it all. One wrong word about their prophet, they'll cut your head off. The Jews have been Chosen so long the joke is old. The Hindus, on the other hand, know it's all happened before and will happen again and there's no point getting excited. Know the fastest growing consumer of energy on the planet, per capita?'

'China?'

'Saudi and the Gulf states. The producers. They want highways and air-conditioned malls and desalination plants to water their golf courses and soon they won't have any spare oil to sell. Then I'll head for the hills of Costa Rica. That's where I met my crazy Balkan girl. Educated, intelligent woman. She'd been working on a cruise liner as a lounge waitress and stopped off in San Juan with a local guy she'd met on board. Ended up in a slummy hood, alone, with a kid. So, she started selling it.'

'The prostitute who wasn't.'

'Everybody has a story. Very fine person. I love her. That's the way it is. She's my wife, I suppose, in the sense that I'm dedicated to her. Where she goes, I go. I accommodate myself to her. I'm as undemanding as possible. Is that not love? To want what's good for someone else? She went back to Europe. When I turned up, she was suspicious.

Until she realised I wasn't some creep. Made it clear I was seeing other women, willing to resume financial support. Well, my crazy Balkan Queen wants to go to Paris now, so that's the end of this town. She wants the kid to get a decent education. He thinks I'm just a kind uncle.'

'What about the other four?'

'Taking them along. Three of them. There's one I'm leaving behind. You should have her. You seem like a nice guy. The expense is minimal. Nineteen years old. Beautiful ass. She's not a prostitute. She ran away from home. I help her out. Did you order that?'

The waiter had brought another vodka.

'I don't remember.'

'The thrill of imminent fatherhood. An uncertain venture. Wait, I have a photo here somewhere of this girl.'

The little thing's umbilical cord was looped around his neck and he would be delivered by caesarean as soon as his mother went into labour.

'Don't know where I put that photo. Finish your drink. My place is across the road.'

I knocked back the drink and went to the toilet. When I returned Sol had paid the bill. As I'd hoped he would.

We left the restaurant. The heat off the baked concrete was a shock to the lungs. It came up through the soles of my shoes as we crossed the street. Cars whished past, flashing in the sun. Their metal skins looked too hot to touch. What were people doing, rushing about on the surface of burning asphalt? The city made a grinding sound, like a badly tuned machine. The fastidious had abandoned town and the subnormal element had grabbed the steering. My collar was soaked as we entered the hall of Sol's building.

A standard socialist-era block. He had not lied about his disdain for the fruits of Babylon. We rode the lift up to the fourth floor.

The apartment was a little cooler than the street, thanks perhaps to the labouring of a defective air-conditioning unit. But the windows were all shut and the air was terribly stale. It seemed absurd to be rich and to breathe such air, and I was disappointed too with the narrow untidy hall, cramped with landlord's furniture, and the boxy living room. I only had his word for it that he had money and I wondered at myself for my credulity. His bookshelves held a few paperbacks; John Grisham and Dan Brown in swollen airport editions. The remaining shelf-space was filled with every kind of vitamin and dietary supplement. He took off his shirt and sat down in front of a screen. He was an egg-shaped hill, his body covered with a halo of white-grey fuzz, even his shoulders. He clicked through an archive of photographs. Hundreds, thousands, of naked girls, sometimes two or three of them together, flickered upon the screen. I was dizzy from the exhausted air.

'Any vodka?'

'I don't do alcohol.'

'Why the pictures?'

He shrugged.

'Someday it might be all I got.'

I pulled up a chair and watched over his hairy shoulder. He was not a good photographer and it was the bones I noticed, particularly the ribs. I noticed bad lighting, awkward poses, birthmarks and other minor physical defects. I recognised the shabby apartment I was now sitting in and imagined them breathing that stale air. I was reminded of medical textbooks and the readers' wives sections of ancient pornographic magazines. But then, unexpectedly, some of the photographs were good and it was like sunlight. In fact, mostly the girls seemed relaxed and trusting. Perhaps he meant no harm, and they took his money and forgave him his misshapen head and his confusions. Other photos were open cunts, sometimes dripping his seed. A picture of a very pretty girl came up, just her face, and I asked him to hold it there. Her lids were heavy, almost closed, her cheeks softly flushed, an expression of serenity, or as though she were on the verge of weeping from too much happiness. I couldn't understand. Was she drugged? Or did he really massage tenderly until the anxiety left the flesh? I thought of the Queen of the harem, taking him off to Paris. Did they see him as vulnerable? As a rich fool? Did he really have magic hands, as the old wizard in Switzerland had said?

'She's one of my extras.'

He named the price. I nodded. He was already texting and I didn't ask him to stop. My own phone beeped then and I walked over to the window and read the message. I typed a brief reply and sent it. I looked down on the city. It was trembling in the heat.

Sol was getting a message back.

'She says, da-di-da, mother sick in hospital, da-da-da, might meet you because she's in a fix, da-da-da... These kids, their mothers are always going into hospital. I help her out sometimes, you see.'

'I've got to go, Sol. My son is on the way.'

I mentioned about the baby with the cord around its neck but he didn't seem to hear. I was not likely to see him again, or to meet any of his friends. He was texting back and waved to me but did not get up.

'Good luck! No telling how it'll turn out.'

I was glad to get out of the apartment and to draw a clean breath. Even the hot air of the city and the glaring light was a pleasure then, as I left the building. And my wife was not in labour. The message was to remind me to bring home vanilla ice cream.

Something in the day had changed. The sun was retreating, if only a little, and it was not going to get any hotter. If I could just manage to stay away from the noise and agitation of the worst streets, it would be bearable. A long summer's evening was promised, slowly coming on. I wanted to sit quietly and hold my wife's hand while we waited. I walked slowly in the shade of some trees in the pedestrian area between the residential blocks. Two old ladies were sitting on a bench, both wearing straw sunhats. An old man walked towards me, accompanied by a little boy on a tricycle, pedalling intently along a path dappled by the light falling through the trees. Then, walking ahead of me, a girl in shorts with very long legs. She had been to the beach and got a tan so deep the skin was glowing bronze, and her legs shimmered as she walked.

Dead Dog

He wondered afterwards, trying to figure it out, if he really had heard what sounded in that moment like a tiny scream. It was the end of a long hot summer and he knew he was capable of imagining things.

What he did hear, as he sat at his desk, was a clatter and commotion from his daughter's room. Then he saw the cat shoot through the hall with a white ball of fur in its jaws. He pursued the cat to the kitchen and lunged at her. He slipped. She tumbled and lost her prey. It scurried across the floor briefly. The cat pounced and caught it again then shot past him before he could lift himself off the ground.

He followed the cat to the kid's bedroom and shut the door and tried to corner her. Several times she evaded him. A spare mattress was jammed under the bed and she darted into a gap between the mattress and the wall. He lay on the floor and put his arm in the gap but she withdrew from reach.

He stood up. Every second he wasted, the cat was chewing up the hamster. He was naked except for his undershorts but was sweating. It was still morning. Two south-facing rooms with balconies. The previous owner had enclosed the balconies with double glazing. Greenhouse effect. Even at night it hardly cooled.

He went to the foot of the bed and kicked the mattress full force, repeatedly, towards the wall. The cat's hindquarters appeared as she scrabbled to back out. He gave the mattress a final kick to convince her and she broke free. He seized her. He gripped her neck and choked her. Gaping jaws, needle teeth. Impossible—her mouth was empty. She had swallowed it whole, like a snake. The little creature was alive inside her. Still gripping her neck with his left hand, he poked the fingers of his right hand down her throat to make her regurgitate. She squirmed, eyes popping. Useless. He released her. She flopped on her side, shook her head and lay there, panting. Then he saw the little white ball, just under the bed. He picked it up. It lay neatly in the palm of his hand, eyes open. No blood. Its heart had burst from fear.

He placed the creature on the sawdust in its tank. It lay on its side, motionless, staring upwards. He kneeled on the floor and watched it, begging it to move.

His daughter had started school the previous September and each day had asked when she could have a hamster. He explained that a pet was a responsibility. He would get her one for Christmas, but first she had to learn to get her schoolbag ready the evening before school and each morning dress herself and brush her teeth and hair. They perfected the routine into winter, getting up under electric light and leaving the house at sunrise, and were never late for school. Right after Christmas he took her to a pet shop and she chose a four-week-old Asiatic dwarf hamster. It would grow no larger than a mouse. She sat silently beside him on the bus home, cradling the box containing her new pet, who she had immediately named Freddie. The cage from the pet shop was too small so he rummaged through the junk on the garret floor of his apartment block. The top floor had originally been servants' quarters, but for decades the residents had used it as a dump. He found a huge home-made aquarium; a roughly welded steel frame with thick glass sides. He lugged it down the service stairs to the apartment and scrubbed it clean and grouted the edges so that dirt would not lodge. The kid arranged sawdust and an exercise wheel and water bottle and released the hamster into its new home. Later they added stones and pieces of wood and a cow's skull. Freddie used the skull as a burrow and slept in the cranial cavity.

After several minutes on his knees, begging the hamster to come back to life, it twitched. Then it got up and walked slowly and stiffly to its refuge inside the skull.

A heavy metal grille covered the top of the tank. There was no way the cat could have reached the bottom of the tank with its paw. It was impossible. It was as though the cat had walked through the glass, like a ghost. And the little scream? Had he really heard it?

He got off his knees and picked up the cat and took her through the kitchen and opened the door to the service stairway. He set her down outside. She stretched out and licked herself. He closed the door.

He went back to his desk and sat down. His heart was beating too fast. He had been interrupted while re-reading an email from two weeks earlier, about a road accident a friend had suffered in India. He had not heard from her since.

He had met her over three and a half years before, after the divorce. He had paid her to come several mornings a week to help him coax his then three-year old kid into her winter clothes and take her across town to her playschool, located near where he had lived with the child's mother. He would make tea for her and it was good to have her company before she left with the child. Over the months and years, though he resisted it, they had become very close. She liked to travel. There were many departures, shorter and longer. He sat in his chair and followed her journeys. There had been no rupture, but she had gone away again. Initially to France, to work. And after a month—surprise—to India. She was unpredictable, but that was another of the things he loved about her. She described arriving in Delhi—coloured saris, tuk-tuks, and a bus in the Himalayas, meeting a friend, buying a bike…

Then—the message he had been puzzling over when disturbed—descriptions of the hard cycling in the mountains, traffic, and hitting a hole in the road. Crashing to the asphalt and ending up in a foreign hospital with a damaged hand and a bruised face.

I was stupidly impatient, after 3 days I got back on the bike. Hell—stress, fear, terrible pain, traffic, and unsure on the bike… maybe it sounds melodramatic… now I don't know… I'm giving it two days to make a plan and will only continue if I'm completely well… which will take time… I'm sad and discouraged. Maybe I'll stay in India and travel around on my own, or get a plane back to the comfort of Bucharest. Maybe it'll be more amusing when I tell you about it in person.

He looked up from the screen. From the next room the hamster was whirring on his wheel. Nothing to worry about.

He dressed and went upstairs to the attic level. He found another heavy metal grille, identical to the first. He brought it down to the kitchen, undressed down to his underwear, and spent thirty minutes cleaning the encrusted dirt from it with a rag and soapy water. He put it on the hamster's tank, above the first grille. It added five centimetres in height and further restricted the cat's manoeuvrability. It had to be impossible now. But it had been impossible before too so he still did not trust it. The cat was malevolent. Unwelcome thoughts had made themselves at home over the long summer, along with a creeping paranoid intuition that his friends were avoiding him. This made no sense— everybody had fled the August heat. But, sweating in the city, broke, waking in the night and turning over the sodden pillow, the mood was stubborn, as was the suspicion that all he had put down in words had been a mistake. He had burned through the last of his money finishing a book. His agent ignored his emails, like an ex-lover who had moved on to more satisfying things. The trickle of paying jobs had dried up in the summer lull. Everyone was at the beach.

A knock on the door.

He put on trousers and a T-shirt.

Mrs Gurau, from the first floor. She was one of the three widows. The block had six apartments, three facing the street and three at the rear. The three apartments at the back had lost their husbands. Mrs Gurau stated the problem. The girl who lived in the one of the houses in the yard had complained of a smell coming from a cellar at the back of the block. The cellar belonged to Mrs Gurau, so...

The dog, he said.

Mrs Marinescu's dog. Mrs Marinescu lived across the hall from him.

Mrs Marinescu had knocked on his door the previous evening. Had he seen her dog? It had been gone for days. It had run away and she had searched the neighbourhood. He felt sorry for the old woman. But the dog crapped in the yard, practically on their doorstep. Mrs Marinescu was a cultivated lady. She had a photograph on her piano of the boyish King Mihai, from just before the communists forced him to abdicate. But she wasn't up to cleaning up after the dog. She had difficulty with the stairs and lowered containers on a string with food and water down to the old animal. Also, it was a big barking beast and it scared the kid. He had been glad to see the yard stay clean for a few days. The half-blind, arthritic dog was another of those things, along with the smashed stairwell windows and the façade that had lost its plasterwork and the broken drainpipes and the attic junk.

He had initiated improvements and repairs in the building since moving in the previous summer—he had needed to in order to get his own apartment habitable and watertight. The neighbours had come to see him as someone you could rely upon—and maybe as a sucker.

He got his torch and followed Mrs Gurau down the stairs.

The smell was perceptible from the bottom of the service stairway.

The ground floor was a series of neglected rooms.

Another junkyard, but darker and even dirtier than the attic. Gas and water pipes snaked beneath the low ceiling of the corridor. He proceeded deeper into the gloom, past open doorways. The first room he passed received dim light through a small dirty window and housed a furnace and boiler, out of use for many decades. From the time when the building functioned according to a plan. From the architect's first drafts, the block had been conceived of as a coherent unit. There had been servants, a watchman and someone to tend the furnace in winter. That was in the 1930s, as the world disintegrated. The men who made the building had been Jews, and Jewish families had lived there first. This was the city's old Jewish neighbourhood, but nothing Jewish remained. Except for a drop of blood in his veins. From the wrong side.

He pressed on slowly, down the unlit corridor, squeezing past broken furniture and lumber stacked along the walls. The smell of decomposition intensified. He reached a metal door, half open. He shone the beam down a steep flight of steps. Perhaps two metres deep. Low buzz of flies. He filled his lungs and descended, holding his breath. The flies got louder. A tiny space. A cellar for coal or wood, provisioned through a chute from the yard. He shone the torch on the dog. He could not see the flies but they sounded huge. He looked up at the chute. Too steep to climb down. The dog had tumbled.

Halfway back up the steps, he drew a breath.

He went out into the brightness of the yard, where Mrs Gurau was waiting.

At the rear of the building the smell was indeed noticeable. There were two small houses at the back of the yard. A middle-aged couple occupied one, their daughter the other, and her front door was a few paces from the chute. The hatch to the chute had disappeared. Now it was a hole, irregular about the edges.

They knocked on the doors of the houses. No answer.

The yard was paved except for a small strip of dirt at the back where a sour plum tree grew beside the wreck of a 1980s Dacia car belonging to the dead husband of crazy Mrs Tudor on the second floor. Not much room there for burying a dog, and in any case the residents might find that idea objectionable. He commented that there was a skip a few streets down outside a tenement of Gypsy families, but he would need help hauling the dog. It would have to be done swiftly and discreetly. No, said Mrs Gurau, You don't want to get beaten up. He nodded. She was right. Disposing of the body where kids played, the summer heat, things turning nasty, police car slowing down to investigate.

They would have to pay someone, like the year before with the other dog. The people from the houses had dealt with that, Mrs Gurau said. Perhaps they had a number. Best wait.

He went upstairs, infected by the air of the little cellar, and threw his clothes on the laundry pile. He showered but afterwards had no underwear. He owned three pairs in total. He located the boxers he had worn the day before. Pale streaks of dried sweat on the dark fabric. He put them on. The other two pairs of shorts he put in the bucket in the bath, along with some T-shirts. He ran the tap, added detergent, and left it to steep. Immediately he began to sweat again. One day he would get builders to remove the windows from the greenhouse balconies. But first he needed underwear.

He sat down at his desk. An email from his publisher. His editor.

Well, his ex-publisher, his ex-editor. Very sorry, can't get behind this item. This reason, that reason, da-di-da. Not unexpected. But still. He thought of the editor, sitting in his smug corporate office overlooking a park, in clean underwear. But that wasn't right. It was his own fault for not buying underwear when things were going well. He did not want to end up like Louis-Ferdinand Céline, in that interview from the 1950s, in his shabby coat, looking like a man who could never get warm, bitching about his finances. I'm too sensitive, said Céline, for the world. After spending the war condemning the Jews, even as they were loaded onto the wagons for their final journey. A doctor, a man of letters, a lover of cats.

So, he had written a dead-end book. Boo-hoo. Not like he was being sent to the Gulag. But it had been a lengthy operation and he had painted himself into a tight corner, financially and mentally, and the problem remained of what to do with the rest of his life.

He wandered into his daughter's room. The cat was stretched over the double-grille, waiting. The hamster was in its cranium. The cat made him nervous.

Three and a half years before, the child's mother announced she had found somebody else and he moved with the kid to a rented room on an upper floor of an apartment block by a busy road. Kitchen, living room and bedroom all in one. He scrabbled to get money together for something better, but also out of fear of the ex's lawyer and the coming custody battle. When making such a determination, the authorities assessed the conditions the child was being raised in. The kid wanted a cat. He explained that cats need space. He got her a goldfish.

At weekends he and the little girl would stroll in what they called cat streets—quieter areas with trees and old houses where cats sat on walls and slunk out from under parked cars. Perhaps one day they would live on a cat street, he told her. In the end the ex decided not to haul him through the courts. After two years he and the kid got the new apartment. It was a ruin. They were still drilling the walls for the electrics and plumbing when they moved in. But they lived on a cat street.

And one morning in early summer, the kid had called him from her grandparents' place outside the city. She had gone out to pick cherries and heard a kitty mewling among the grapevines. Could she keep it? But it came from a line of vicious ferals or else was just psychotic. For weeks they were covered with scratches. The freedom of the stairways and the upper floor was insufficient to burn off her manic aggression. The young cat was crazy to kill things. Unnatural gurglings rose from her throat when she spied pigeons outside the window.

One evening, when the kid was at her grandparents' again, the kitten stepped out the open window and strolled along the sill three floors above the street. He went to fetch her back. She tried to turn but slipped. He watched her tumble through the air, bounce off a parked car and hit the footpath. She mewled and ran under the car. He pulled on his trousers and ran downstairs, bare-chested. She crawled

out from under the car, whining. He picked her up gently
and carried her back upstairs and set her on his mattress
and lay beside her, stroking her fur. There was some blood
about her nose and he was still not sure she would not die.
He thought about having to tell the little girl. The kitten
lay there, stunned and bruised, replaying the reel of its
plunge. She had not learned incrementally, from falling
from branches, having been scared to enter the yard ruled
by the dog. Then, within minutes, she began to purr. He
watched the kitten and composed the story for the little
girl, with a happy ending.

The kitten was subdued for the rest of the evening. And
whatever way she had whacked her head improved her
slightly. The scratches on their arms healed.

He washed the steeping laundry, wrung it out and draped
it on the bathroom radiator for when he got back.

He set off on foot through the glaring streets and in
twenty minutes reached her block. He went to the second
floor and let himself in. Her apartment was an oven. He had
shut all the windows against sudden summer storms. He
took off his shoes then opened the windows on the enclosed
balcony off the living room, the windows in her bedroom
and the kitchen windows. It was a standard communist-
era block, but bright and uncluttered. She had inherited it
from a deceased aunt the previous year. The country was
emptying, its population thinning out, and all you had to
do was pass the time until you inherited real estate. She
had made it her own by decorating it with things she had
found—giant dried leaves, ornate branches, a huge piece of
bark decorated with blue and red and gold children's paints.

He drank a glass of water then undressed completely. He went to the bathroom and put his underwear in the washing machine, with the load prepared on his previous visit, five days before. He set the dial and turned the washing machine on. When it was done, he would strip the bed from the last Airbnb booking and leave that in the machine until he came again. He checked the guests in and out and made sure they had coffee and clean sheets.

He took down the sheets and towels washed on his previous visit from the lines on the enclosed balcony. He folded them and put them in the wardrobe in the bedroom. Using a plastic bottle filled from the kitchen tap, he watered all the plants. She had many plants and, in strange coloured bottles set on windowsills and on dressers, she also had cuttings that had put out roots and continued to grow. He had not let anything die.

He cleaned the bathroom and the kitchen surfaces. He dusted in all the rooms. He washed the floor.

On his first visit after she had left he had found three crisp one-hundred euro notes on the kitchen table. A loan. He was grateful. He had been broke for some time and presumed she was short of money too, travelling to pick fruit in the French countryside. When she phoned and said the season was over, that she had arrived too late to find work he was sorry for her and thought of the money she had left him. Then she phoned again a few weeks after that and told him about India. He did not understand. But he was happy for her.

He sat naked on the sofa, turning this over. After a long time he went to check the dial on the washing machine. It had hardly moved. He walked back to the living room. A full-length mirror was propped against the wall opposite the doorway. He looked at himself. His skin was pale. He had not left the city all summer. He was not old yet but he was getting there. To pass the time he did a series of yoga stretches on the linoleum floor. Then sit-ups and press-ups. He took a cloth from the sofa and folded it on the floor and placed a cushion on it and sat cross-legged and straight-backed and did his breathing exercises. He had been to India too and had studied these things. He had even learned some Sanskrit. Serious guy. That was all a decade before. But he was sure he had not learned to meditate. All he had learned was to sit still for long enough to observe how his head buzzed.

He showered then sat on the sofa again and listened to the washing machine.

He went to her bedroom. Her bed was a mattress on the floor. He lay down and wondered when she was coming back. One of David Berman's songs played in his head. A tune called 'All My Happiness Is Gone'. He had listened to it over and over on Youtube. It played that trick of putting heartbroken words to a cheerful melody.

David Berman had died weeks before, on another continent. He was the same age as David. The first time he met him was at a festival in a provincial Romanian town. He had given David a present of tinned carp. Carp is *crap* in Romanian and that was written on the tin. He gave the poet a can of crap and David said, When I get back to Nashville I'll put it on top of your books. David had read his books and he had listened to David's music. One of the most talented people he had ever met. The last album had been his suicide note. In which he confessed he was barely hanging on. He could not stop listening to it. The songs were so good. He thought of his own talent and the dead-end book, how he would keep going. If he should keep going. The problem was that he did not know how to stop making things from the junk of his experience.

He closed his eyes and folded his hands over his chest and soon he was thinking of her touch and how he felt when he was inside her and how her face became in stages ever more beautiful when they made love. She would close her eyes and disappear into herself in these moments. And that was good, because he did not want to think of her seeing his flushed and grimacing face. Minutes passed, lying there, and he became hard. He touched himself slowly and felt her close and it was happiness again.

He showered a second time. He felt grateful for something but was unsure what. The washing machine entered the overexcitement of the spin-dry cycle. He went back to the sofa and sat there until it finished. Then he took the sheets and towels and hung them from the lines in the balcony. He put on his clean, still damp boxers. He stripped the mattress and put the sheets and pillowcases and towels in the washing machine, ready for his next visit, in six days' time unless there was a booking to attend to sooner. He drank more water, dressed, locked up and walked home.

A knock on the door. Trousers and T-shirt back on.

A pretty girl in her twenties. Andra, from the house with its front door near to the chute. She had just got back from the beach, she said, and the smell was terrible. Yes, he replied, the dog was down there. She believed her parents had a telephone number. But they were on holiday. She would call them.

Ten minutes later they stood in the hot yard. He, Mrs Gurau, Andra and her boyfriend. The boyfriend was quiet. He supported his partner by standing right behind her. Andra had the number now from her parents. They agreed there was no point trying to get money out of Mrs Tudor, who went out in the hallway when subjected to renovation noise or cuts in water supply and screamed at the top of her lungs. You could also exclude the three young people who rented Apartment 1—they had just moved in. The talk circled and the call waited to be made. You took the initiative, you owned the problem. Andra dictated the number to Mrs Gurau. She tried calling but no answer. So he tried calling on his phone. A woman answered. He wondered what to say. It was not like ordering a pizza. It was awkward to announce to a stranger that you needed a rotting dog removed.

Incineration? 150 lei. Transport? Another 550—it was outside the city. Somebody would be over later. Goodbye.

He agreed to gather the cash.

Expensive. But spirits were up. They were a team.

The cat followed him back up the stairs. He went inside and stripped to his shorts. The woman on the phone had been professional. A service for the bereft pet owner, who would be spoken to softly and charged accordingly. What did humans cost to bury? Nothing obviously, in some circumstances. He had envisioned for the dog a couple of taciturn Gypsies, cigarettes in the corners of their mouths, with a supermarket trolley or a hand-pulled cart. And there were enough junkies in a one-kilometre radius to pull dog-corpses out of basements if you caught them in the right moment. Where were they when you needed them? Sitting in cellars themselves, chewing their fingers.

He was hungry. The thing with the cat that morning had made him forget breakfast. He sat down and ate bread and tomatoes and cheese. The phone rang. He wiped his fingers, expected it would be the animal funerary service. A weak male voice, from several streets away.

Hi, can you come?

Could he come? What was wrong?

Not on the phone, please. Can you come now, please?

Yes, he could come right away.

First he went to the kid's bedroom. The cat lay on the grille, waiting. He picked her up and went through the kitchen and put her out. He was not going to leave her alone with the hamster until he could observe her next attempts. He did not believe the cat could now do harm. But he did not believe what he believed either. It was getting like that with a number of things.

He put his damp clothes back on and headed out.

The heat of the day was at its peak. The streets were deserted. He walked in shade where that was possible but generally it was not. In five minutes he reached his friend's house. An old single-level building with an unkempt garden of fruit trees and straggling redcurrant bushes and weeds.

The previous summer he had helped his friend move there from another house after quarrels with the landlord. It had been a hot morning and his friend was drunk. On the second trip in the car, his friend, from the passenger seat, waved his hand at the people beneath the sun and slurred,

This is a stupid place, these people have no wisdom. His friend was from India but was a naturalised American citizen and had assumed licence to cast such stones. He had thought to reply, And who will teach them? You?

But he did not speak. A week after that, sitting in the leafy shade of the new yard, his friend confided he had a problem. At first he had thought that it was a minor stroke that had caused him to drag his left leg. But he had done tests and the problem appeared to be due to a degenerative motor neurone condition. It affected his coordination.

He chose this moment to vent his irritation at his friend, but covered it by speaking softly.

Listen, he said, you have this beautiful place to live, you can earn a living, you have a woman who loves you. One unlucky drunken fall and you're on the next plane, back to your brother in LA. You have to take care of yourself. The drinking, the smoking…

He would later regret chiding the suffering man, when he should have had a heart and listened.

The trees shook loose their leaves and winter came with a sharp north wind, and he was woken in the night by the phone. It was four AM.

I can't get up. I'm on the ground and I can't get up, said the voice at the other end.

His friend had got up to go to the bathroom and his legs had folded beneath him. The door to his house was locked. The landlord, who had a spare key, was not answering his phone.

Stay warm, pull your quilt over yourself. Bundle some clothing or a sheet and piss into that if you have to. Stay comfortable until dawn until I can get to you.

While they were talking his friend managed to haul himself back into bed.

For the next couple of days he ran about, obtaining his friend's medical records from the United States, printing them out, trying over a holiday weekend to get an appointment with a neurologist. His friend had never learned to speak the language of the country. He drove him to the consultation and waited in the hall. It lasted forty-five minutes and the doctor's breezy attitude afterwards—rushing away, back to her own life—told him his friend was not dying. Not that day or the next. He needed physical therapy to regain motor function and muscle tone and to have continued tests. He could not see his friend doing these things. And his medical insurance was valid only in the United States.

Driving him back to his house, he asked, What did the doctor tell you?

Stop smoking, drinking.

You said?

Eh-eh.

A little nasal eh-eh. Barely audible, and a tiny shake of his head.

They drove on in silence. He did not like his friend any more. He wished him gone, back to America, where he could be treated and where his wealthy brother would ensure his comforts. He wanted his friend to disappear.

The door to the house was open and he stepped into the shade of the porch and called out. A small man in his fifties emerged from the bedroom, shaven-headed, stub of a rolled cigarette between his fingers. He wore a smart short-sleeved cotton indigo shirt, but he was shrunken and wasted, shuffling about in a pair of old loafers. The backs of the shoes had been crushed down and softened so they were like slippers. They looked uncomfortable, but he had become habituated. Fifteen years had passed since they had first met, in a night club. An attractive guy in interesting clothes who said he was a photographer from New York.

I'm leaving. I have a flight at midnight.

This is sudden.

Alina.

Really he was saying Adina, but his speech had deteriorated. Adina was his woman friend. But he had an ex called Alina who he had been in love with for years. And probably still was. And because he still spoke of her often it was frequently unclear which woman he was in fact referring to. Everything having become confused in his speech and his head, it was no easy matter. But in this case it was Adina.

It's the end here.

He had wished to be done with him and now that it was happening he felt uneasy, as though he had wished for his death. Or at least not to witness the spectacle.

I... I...

He hobbled about, searching through his round Ghandi-glasses.

I...

He located his pouch of rolling tobacco on the table and picked it up. He looked at it and put it down and picked up a water glass half-full with red wine and drank from that. Then he addressed himself to the cigarette. He had a little apparatus that rolled them perfectly, with a filter. He lit up. That's over. So.

I'm sorry, he said. He was sorry, and also glad that this inevitable disaster of the heart had finally occurred, and disgusted that he was glad, judging fate like a doctor or a stranger.

Adina had a girl of nine and a boy of four. She worked alternate months in Vienna, nursing an elderly woman. Her mother took care of the children when she was away. The kids' father had run off, gone abroad. He was not in contact and sent no money. Adina had been beautiful once, but the years were hard, and there were worries about money and her kids. One day she and his friend had got chatting on social media and he said, I'd like to take your picture. This was his routine. He photographed women. He used fabrics and tricks with lighting and filters and he made them beautiful. They would take their clothes off to be beautiful through his lens. She replied, You did that years ago. He had forgotten. They had briefly been together, some fifteen or sixteen years before. Then he was with Adina again.

He had his catering business. An underground restaurant run from home, with regular clients. Semi-private parties with spicy, fragrant dishes and a warm atmosphere. Bright incoherent decor suggestive of Eastern spirituality. There was a statuette of Shiva and another of Buddha, though he was neither Hindu nor Buddhist. He was Sikh, without the turban. His parents had sold a swathe of land in the Punjab and sent him to flight school in Texas, and for years he had flown commercial airliners. He maintained a large file of photographs on his laptop of naked female flight attendants, taken in hotel rooms on stopovers in various US cities. He had married a Swiss woman who worked for the United Nations and they lived in Manhattan. He became a photographer and had a file of pictures of famous people, from Boutros Boutros-Ghali to Jennifer Lopez. After his wife divorced him, early in the century, he came to Bucharest on a photographic assignment. He slept with many women in a short period of time and figured it was a good place to settle. For a while he worked taking stills on the sets of pornographic films. Finally he relied on his cooking. His ventures had a limited span and folded with a dispute with a partner or a visa problem or the end of a relationship or family matters that required a trip to India or LA. Money slipped though his fingers. His LA brother paid for flights, bailed him out, and there were loans from well-wishers, not always repaid.

Adina reckoned if they could grow the home-catering business together she could stop shuttling off to Vienna and be with the kids. But the business did not grow. Now in addition to the invalid in Vienna she had one in Bucharest. She did his work.

He remembered drinking with his friend late one evening, after a catering party. The money was counted and Adina was clearing up. His friend lifted his right arm and mumbled something to Adina. She smiled, hurried to where he was seated, thinking he was offering her an embrace at the end of the day's work. Too late, awkwardly half-embracing him from a standing position, she realised he was pointing. He wanted her to fetch his tobacco pouch, from the table several paces away. She gave him his tobacco and continued clearing up.

Now the ex-pilot was taking his final flight, booked and paid for by the LA brother, and at midnight he would take off. Perhaps he would doze and wake over Greenland and gaze out the window. And then he would be among the southern Californian palms, and no more pretending at being a man among women.

I have to go now, he told his friend, after they had talked a little. There are a couple of things I have to do. The kid is coming back soon. The grandparents are bringing her back.

Oh. Oh. Yes.

His friend gestured helplessly with his hands. Abandoned again.

They wished each other luck.

After the shade of the house the light was harsh. He began walking down the middle of the street. No cars. There was nobody. He would not see his friend again. He had got what he wished for and that assailed him. And then there was somebody, from nowhere. A man's voice. He turned around and the young man waved. He slowed but did not stop entirely as the stranger hurried to catch up with him. It was a city where it was not prudent to engage too easily. Though occasionally only directions were needed.

Are you from around here?

He waved his hand noncommittally. Maybe, maybe not.

Sorry to bother… walking around all day… divorce…. custody hearing later… need to get cleaned up… a haircut… if you can spare it… so I can go to a barber's… thirty-five lei.

Unfeigned desperation. Short beard and decent clothes, with just a note of dishevelment. He even had a smart little leather satchel over his shoulder. A hipster in distress. But a custody hearing. Kicked when you were down. He knew that threat. He had barely escaped, back when he was living in the little room with the kid. It did not go to court in the end. But he would never forget the feeling. His left hand went into the pocket with the wallet. It would be a relief to empty it of the entire sum and feel holy for a moment. He glanced back at his friend's house. But beyond that, at the end of the street, was another kind of house. After visiting it the junkies, the most emaciated ones, would sometimes be in a hurry. You'd see one on the street corner, trousers around his knees, looking for a vein. Then there was the dead dog. He needed one-hundred lei. He only had eighty-five. And a haircut didn't cost thirty-five lei. A cheap one cost fifteen. He needed a haircut himself.

Can't help you.

He walked away, knowing the thing about the custody hearing could well be true. Two minutes later the phone rang. The sympathetic woman from the pet-cremation service. The van would be along at six.

He reached his block and entered. The cat appeared. He reached down to stroke her and she tried to bite him. Not that she resented being strangled. Just that she liked to bite. He let himself and the cat into the apartment. He undressed and drank some water. He fed the cat.

He thought of his friend, gathering his belongings for the flight. They had spent an evening together, a couple of weeks before. All other friends having left the city. He had gone to his leafy yard towards sunset, sprayed himself against the mosquitoes swarming down from the trees and lit the barbeque. He had brought the food. He cooked pork loins stuffed with prunes and reduced a sauce of honey and balsamic vinegar and served it up. They ate outside, mosquito coils burning under the table to protect their exposed feet. His friend hardly spoke during the meal as darkness fell and when he did it was a lazy mumble. The right side of his mouth was paralysed. He could hardly cut the meat. But later, after enough wine, he began to reminisce. He dipped in and out of memories and the identities of people were confused. The narrative of his life was sinking out of view. He began a strange monologue, rambling but finally animated. A story about his days as a pilot in America, a stopover in Montana, a motel, a woman. She had her period and they covered the white sheets with blood. There were red handprints on the sheets. It looked like a murder scene. And the look the Mexican maid gave them in the morning when they came back from breakfast. The accomplishment verified by a third party. And then in the Hilton. It took a moment for the listener to realise, but the theme had been transposed to another decade, another city, another woman. This time expensive chocolates, eating them out of her ass in the classy hotel room, and the chocolate getting all over the sheets. Again, the filthy look from the maid in the morning. What did it mean? His old friend's hands trembled as he rolled a cigarette. He could have let him continue emptying his storeroom of erotic victories, in fascinated complicity with the bizarre dreamscape unfolding, but the reality of the broken mind and body before him made it painful. He rose and cleared away the dishes to the kitchen and washed them—his friend was unsteady even for light carrying—and said goodnight.

He sat at his desk but it was useless to try to write. It would need another kind of day to write words that brought no money. He was short fifteen lei.

There were a few hours left until they came for the dog.

He put on old ripped jeans and pulled a clean but old T-shirt over his sticky-damp skin. A broken air-conditioning unit had lain for over a year in the stairway on the floor beneath his, outside his neighbours' door. The couple with jobs. He was in advertising, she was a newsreader. He had been in their home once. Immaculate. They did not tolerate dust. The effort ended at their doorway. When he had volunteered to shift the unit the husband explained he could not help. Bad ligaments.

The unit weighed perhaps less than forty kilos. But it was awkwardly shaped and there was nothing to grip except the metal struts on one side where it had been affixed to a wall. These cut into his fingers. He could only move it a few centimetres at a time, across the hallway to the stairs, leaning over it, sweat dripping from the tip of his nose. He paused to catch his breath at the top of the stairs. Two flights down a once-elegant curving art-deco stairway. Some of the windows to the tiny interior courtyard were broken and the rest were encrusted with dirt. The plaster on the walls was flaking and the remaining paint peeling away. But he did not want to scrape or chip the steps by mishandling the unit.

He set to work. He stood with his left foot two steps below the unit and his right foot three steps below pulled it gently until one end rested on his left thigh. He moved his hands to support it beneath, withdrew his left foot and slowly lowered the unit until it rested diagonally on the edge of several steps. Then he pulled it straight, so that it stood on end. This revolved the unit ninety degrees from its initial position. By repeating this manoeuvre, he was in effect rolling it down the stairs. It was more difficult where the stairway curved. After each roll he rested and wiped each side of his face against the shoulders of his wetT-shirt. The sweat ran into his eyes.

He kept going until he had the unit in the yard. He climbed the stairs slowly for his car keys. Then he rolled the unit through the yard, into the street, to the back of an estate car, a twenty-year-old Subaru Forester. The letters had fallen off the back so it was just a *RU*. A second-hand mistake, acquired in a moment of ambition. With a final effort, he loaded the unit into the car. He stood there for a moment, muscles aching, welts across the insides of his fingers, dizzy from the heat.

He put the back seats of the car down then went to the ground floor of the apartment building, entering from the service doorway beside the main entrance, into the rooms and tunnels smelling of decomposition, and rummaged for more manageable scrap. He found sections of an old drainpipe and loaded those into the car. Then he went up to the attic and gathered lengths of rusty piping, metal canisters, a broken car jack and various unidentifiable mechanical parts. Five trips up and down the stairs. Finally, he filled sacks with some of the dusty bottles hoarded in various boxes throughout the attic. Glass was not worth much, but ten kilos would buy a loaf of bread.

It was too hot to sit in the car so he put down all the windows and stood outside by the open driver's door for a couple of minutes. Then he sat in and started the engine. It was still too hot to breathe. The steering wheel burned his hands. The air conditioning did not work. Two summers before, the AC belt had snapped and got snagged in the engine belt and destroyed the motor. He had replaced the motor but judged it smart not to invest in a new AC belt.

He pulled out. The car was not taxed or insured but the scrap yard was nearby. It was an indeterminate neighbourhood. There were tidy residential streets just to the north and signs of wealth, but the order frayed suddenly towards his own street. You could not say if the trend was towards renovation or decay. There were conflicting signs, including the appearance of betting shops, a pawnbroker's, car repair workshops, a scrapyard.

He pulled into the scrapyard and a man in overalls guided him as he reversed towards the electronic scales, a four or five square metre aluminium platform twenty centimetres above the ground. He got out and did the bags of glass first. Then the metal. The man in overalls helped him with the AC unit. It was weightless done like that. The metal came to over sixty kilos. Another man came out of a hut and handed him thirty-eight lei and nodded. Thank-yous were not part of the routine. But he said thank-you to the man.

As he pulled out of the yard he saw the three men, waiting, as if they had been there forever. Two had shopping trolleys and the other a two-wheeled metal handcart. Each had scrap metal and bottles of plastic and compacted cans. Had they been there all along? Had he just driven past them? If he had jumped the queue, been waved ahead, they seemed not to care. They waited their turns, each with one hand on their load, as though keeping it safe. And he had felt sorry for himself, getting into his overheated car with its history of trouble.

He drove back and parked and went up to the apartment. He undressed and showered under cool water. Afterwards he put on one of the pairs of boxers he had washed earlier. A soft breeze moved through the apartment. It was merciful but not enough to disperse the gathered heat. He had a little free time now, but his thoughts were too scattered and fragile. He thought of washing the floor. Then he remembered.

He wrote a message to his neighbour below, the household where they both had jobs, asking for money for the dead dog. Then he put on clean trousers and a clean T-shirt and went and knocked on Mrs Marinescu's door and told her the dog was dead. She told him how she had found it when it was a puppy. It had turned up at the gate, lost, after her husband had died. The poor little thing had an injured leg, maybe from a car, and that was why it always limped. He was very sorry, but now the dog was in the basement and had to be removed and it cost money. She went to her kitchen and came back with three crisp hundred lei bills. He understood she was offering as much as she had, because it was her dog, and that under normal circumstances she would have paid the entire sum. He knew she had no children to help her and only two piano students left, for as long as she could keep that up. She had fallen in the winter and hurt her right hand. He gave one hundred lei back to her. Taking two hundred from her would let him keep it down to a hundred for each other household. He went down and knocked on Andra's door.

She offered three hundred, for herself and her parents, but he gave her a hundred back. Then he went to Mrs Gurau and she handed him two hundred, but he told her he would give a hundred back when he got it from the neighbour with a job. He skipped the young people who rented and crazy Mrs Tudor who would only scream or start talking about the church.

He went back to his apartment and put the money on the desk. He added a hundred of his own to the pile, in small denomination notes, and still had some change left over from the scrap.

He flicked on his laptop and checked his email. One from the neighbour downstairs. And one from India. The first from her in two weeks, since she had hurt her arm. He checked downstairs first.

No problem!

Then he drew a breath and clicked the other one.

Her arm was mended. The hard-working holidaymakers were back in the saddle. Fifty to seventy-five kilometres a day.

… Burning heat, torrential rain, blinding dust, carhorns, trucks, villages full of people staring at you, scooters braking in front of you to get you in a selfie, salvation of restaurants/ canteens with cold juice and something to eat and always the search for a hotel decent enough to get some sleep.

Unfortunately we can't camp, too many people, too few forests. I've been a princess the past few days: wonderful clean hotel, clean bathroom, clean sheets, air conditioning and room service! I imagined you laughing at me. But I really appreciate it. We didn't leave the room all day. David had diarrhoea and I enjoyed the air conditioning and not having to pedal…

And more. About terrible cities, hard cycling, how she was surprised she had lasted a month. She was writing the message on a train to the highlands, to Darjeeling.

He leaned back in the seat. Air conditioning. Clean sheets. The friend had been introduced by name. Since Berman's death he had wished not to meet any more Davids for a while. Presented him while he was in the bathroom, pissing through his ass. Just as she had announced their adventure by tumbling from the bike. Pity us our weak flesh, as we undergo our trials.

The exotic journey was a bizarre parenthesis or else she had left him properly long ago but neglected to mention. Or the wheels were spinning and the blurred landscape scrolling past and her mind undistracted by the possibility of life on other planets. A crazy postcard, garbled by distance. Or he was the lunatic, unable to read the plain signs on the road and incapable now of adding two and one. It was there with the cat walking through the glass or the incomprehensibility of the sudden death of a friend.

The phone rang. A man's voice. The removal service was approaching.

He put on the old trousers and the damp T-shirt he had worn for the scrap and put the torch in his pocket and went downstairs. He stood on the baking footpath as the big black van squeezed into the space behind his own car. The van was new and clean. *Farewell Pet Service* written on the side. A dignified operation. A big man in grey overalls got out and they shook hands. He was middle-aged, overweight and glum. Humiliating work, disposing of carcasses, meeting people who had lost their companions, some of these people old themselves. But better than collecting old bottles. The man opened the doors at the back of the van and removed a black zippered body-bag. The inside of the van smelled of disinfectant and decomposition. The man banged the doors shut and they went into the yard. Andra and the boyfriend were there too. In solidarity perhaps, or just to see it done.

Paperwork, said the big man. By which he meant money. He made out the receipt.

He signed and handed over the cash and the man pocketed it.

He turned on the torch and guided the man down the dark corridor. He wondered had the man seen many such cases. Dilapidated unlit buildings and a corpse rotting in a basement. Surely he had and the smell was nothing strange to him. Perhaps he had been doing it for years. It did not seem fitting to ask. And there was something shameful in hiring a stranger to do such an unclean job. They reached the open door to the cellar and he went down ahead of the man. He shone the torch on the steps for him to follow. The beam from the torch was inadequate. The batteries were low. The man took the steep steps slowly. He looked like a giant under the low ceiling. The smell was intense and the flies buzzed noisily. I can't see anything, said the man. The ground was black. There, he replied, shining the weak beam on the dead dog. The man manoeuvred closer and placed the bag beside the dog. He took a pair of gloves from his overalls and put them on. I have no gloves, he told the man, to excuse himself. The man did not reply. He drew a breath and leaned in, hoisting first the front of the dog over the bag, then its hindquarters. The black bag melded with the dog in the gloom. Then the dog was in and the man zipped the bag closed. He straightened up and drew a short breath. The bag had canvas handles at each end and they carried it up the steps together, the man leading. It was lighter than he had expected. A big dog, but perhaps it seemed bigger alive. Or else, like the air-conditioning unit, effortless when done by two people.

They emerged into the light, watched by the young couple, and carried the dog through the yard, onto the street. They set it down on the footpath and the man opened the van doors. They hoisted it in. The man removed his gloves and threw those into the back of the van too and shut the doors. He nodded, expressionless, then turned to go.

Thank you for your help, he said to the man, who was already walking out of view, to the far side of the van.

Thank you for your help too, came the man's voice. He opened his door and got in. The engine started up.

After the absence of communication and the unreadability of the man's face, the simple courtesy of the reply surprised him. He realised he hadn't been expected to assist with this low task. The man was acknowledging the gesture. He was grateful the man had spoken.

The young couple were still in the courtyard. They had waited, perhaps with a touch of awkwardness for having let him take the lead in disposing of the problem on their doorstep. But they were all free of the dog now, and that was good.

Done, he said.

He was satisfied. He had done what had to be done.

He was walking with his arms a little out from his body, fingers splayed.

I'm going to wash now, he said.

He went upstairs. He had not touched the dog directly but he opened the door with his elbow and closed it behind him with his shoulder. The air of the cellar clung, thick in his nostrils. He still heard the buzzing of the flies. He was sure he would be smelling it and hearing the noise when he woke the next morning. He put the laundry bucket under the tap in the bath and added the detergent. He peeled the clothes off his wet skin and dumped everything in the bucket. It foamed up and he stirred it with his hands. He stepped into the bath and moved the bucket to the far end. He redirected the flow of water from tap to shower. He soaped himself all over. He washed his hair, massaging his scalp hard.

He got out and dried himself. Immediately he began to sweat again. The sun was not as high now. It was a good moment to mop the entire floor. The evaporation would cool the place a little in time for the kid coming home. Not that she ever complained. But it would be a good thing to do.

He put on the last pair of clean underwear. They ripped at the crotch. He arranged himself as best he could. Then the phone rang. The ex's parents, bringing the kid. They would be there in ten minutes.

He made his daughter's bed and swept her bedroom floor. The cat mooched about then jumped up onto the grille above the hamster's cage and sniffed delicately. He picked her off and ejected her into the service stairway.

You're a bad cat, Mitzi.

She slouched away on padded feet. A beautiful, muscular animal, tense and alert. But were she the size of a panther she would play with him then bite his head off.

He went downstairs and stepped out into the yard just as the gate was opening. The light had lost its white glare and was almost pleasant now.

The little girl ran to him and jumped into his arms. She clung to him with her arms and legs like a little monkey. Then he set her down.

Daddy, can we go see a film?

He had twenty-three lei in his pocket.

Not today. We can go to the park. When it gets a little cooler, but before the mosquitoes come out.

The grandfather entered the yard, huffing, bearing two heavy bags loaded with things from their garden and their basement. The kind of reusable fold-out sacks you buy at supermarket check-outs. He had used a number of them to take the bottles to the scrap-yard. His existence was inconvenient to the grandparents. He was an intrusion on the decency and integrity of their family. But they gave him food sometimes. There were apples, cucumbers, eggs, tomatoes, a bottle of plum brandy, and a whole chicken. He inspected it and thanked the grandfather. They said goodbye.

He grasped the handles of the sacks to carry them inside, but the girl cried out:

Look, it's Mitzi!

The cat had poked her head through one of the broken ground-floor windows. She had always been wary of the yard, venturing at most a few paces from the doorway, sniffing the ground and chewing at tufts of greenery sprouting in the cracked paving. To the cat's nose it was dog territory. The dog would see the cat and limp forward, growling, and she would scurry back to safety.

Now she sensed that something had changed. She leapt down from the outer sill and began to investigate the ground, timidly, in the company of the child and the man. Gaining confidence, she went towards the rear of the building, towards the area that had recently been the dog's, circling back sometimes, pausing and lifting her nose to the air, ears and tail quivering, then advancing again.

Come on, Mitzi! said the little girl.

They followed a few paces behind. The cat stopped at the corner of the building, at the hole the dog had fallen into, and sniffed the edges. He told the kid about the dog.

What's down there?

Nothing.

Can we go down and see?

No.

But why did it go there?

When animals die they want to be on their own, away from people and other animals. It was the only place it could go.

They looked into the hole, all three of them. There was nothing to see but a square of blackness. The odour persisted.

I didn't like that dog, said the girl.

I know. I didn't either.

So why are you sad?

Sad?

Your voice is.

I'm tired. I wake up in the night.

The cat moved on. She crept through the courtyard, towards the patch of dirt and the single sour plum tree beside the carcass of the car. She seemed to know all about trees, and had only needed the chance to be reminded. The stupid cat that had tumbled from the windowsill was getting to see something real. She was not a bad cat. She was just a cat. She stopped at the base of the tree, looking up at its black trunk and branches, tensed and primed, her tail quivering.

Look at her! said the child, taking the man's hand. She's a free cat!

When the child was born and he first held her, he felt he was good enough to protect her and do only what was right. That was love, and nothing else held the foolish precarious world together.

The cat coiled back low to the ground, taut as a spring, swished its tail once, and launched itself straight up the trunk, claws gripping the bark with a fast delicate raindrop clatter. She reached the first solid bough and took up position there, arrogantly, looking down at them from among the branches and the leaves, bombarded by manic sunlight, like she had seen it all before in a previous life.

Acknowledgements

The author wishes to gratefully acknowledge the support of the Arts Council of Ireland—the people who work there—during the writing of this book.

WICKLOW COUNTY COUNCIL LIBRARY SERVICE

Author: Ó'Ceallaigh, P   Acc.No.:

Please return this book by the last date shown.
Readers will be charged for lost and damaged books.